Defending the Colonies

A Novel of
Alternate American History

Defending the Colonies

A Novel of
Alternate American History

Daniel H Lessin

ISBN: 978-1-7347976-0-2 (print)
       978-1-7347976-1-9 (ebook)

Interior Design: Patti Frazee
Cover Design: Jason Grossman

Some characters and events in this book are ficticious. Any similarity to real persons, living or dead, is purely coincidental and not intended by the author.

Black Labrador Creations, LLC
Minneapolis, MN

This book is dedicated to adventurers of
the kind with an open heart and an open mind.

A Note to Readers

This book comes with some caveats. *Defending the Colonies* is a work of alternate history. The Revolutionary War did not happen in this fashion. Some of the personalities, locales, and battles are fictional, whilst elements of others are fabricated for lack of information available. The strong language and morally questionable viewpoints taken in this book, meant to be historically correct, do not represent the views of the author.

Though the author personally feels that the Crown forces had relative justice on their side in the American War of Independence, he does not mean to suggest that they were the absolute heroes of the conflict. There were many people of courage and honor on both sides. There were many scoundrels, fools, and incompetents on both sides as well.

chapter 1.
Lexington and Concord

Governor Gage's Mansion, Boston, Massachusetts

March 10, 1775, 7:00 PM

Rarely had Major Giles Finch seen such extravagance at a party. Elegant beeswax candles dotted the path to the military governor's mansion on Fleet Street, newly restored after the lootings of 1765. It was three stories tall, had six chimneys, and was protected by a wrought iron fence and a pair of sentinels, who were taking invitations for their host, the renowned General Thomas Gage.

As the rotund 45-year old engineer dismounted from his horse, he smoothed his uniform with his pudgy fingers and, doffing his hat, scratched his head before handing the reins to a groom. Noting the fancily decorated stagecoaches passing by, Finch shook off a slight feeling of inadequacy and tipped the young lad, who was dressed in handsome livery, though it was caked in mud and smelled of horseflesh.

Finch strode into the building just as a fusillade of

fireworks went off, pyrotechnics being one of Gage's personal fascinations. Yet, as the explosions lit up the sky, the British officers present, as well as a portion of Boston's high society, seemed oblivious to the display. They were too busy mingling over cigars and cider. Gage, chatting idly with his guests alongside his wife, was looking resplendent, studded with more medals and other decorations than could possibly be won in a lifetime.

It is a dangerous gambit, Finch thought, *holding a party in the wake of ravening revolutionaries.* Yet Finch knew that while Gage, a compassionate but stubborn individual, was protected by little more than a small expeditionary force, the governor general was not one to give in to the demands of rabble rousers.

It was in the face of such stubbornness that Finch intended to implore Gage to reconsider his firm stance on the Sons of Liberty, a motley crew of radicals terrorizing Boston and the colonies at large. Revolution brewed on the horizon. Enacting diplomacy with this band was not going to be easy. But in order to keep the peace, Finch felt it was a necessity. He also understood that this event might be his only opportunity to make his case to Gage, even if it meant spoiling the festive atmosphere.

Finch barely took in his surroundings as he entered the ballroom. He rubbed his temples, trying to concentrate amidst the music of an English country dance. Though Finch and his family were longtime residents of Boston, he still yearned for the creature comforts of his native Chelmsford, where his debonair brother Jacob maintained the family home.

Finch had witnessed war in the colonies only 12 years before, and had no desire to reacquaint himself with its horrors. When he was young and foolish, he had yearned for conflict. Back then, his career involved maintaining irrigation canals and repairing forts damaged by Bonny Prince Charlie in the brief but bloody Jacobite Uprisings. But after a tour of duty on the North American continent during the Seven Years War, Finch no longer held any misconceptions that war could be glorious.

As Finch made his way to the punch bowl, he heard a familiar voice call to him.

Whirling around, he caught sight of the gouty, pencil-thin Brigadier General Hugh, Earl of Percy. Bulbous-nosed and with a ready smile, Percy significantly outranked Finch. Nevertheless, the two had spoken amiably on several occasions.

"Finch." Percy spoke evenly, his hand extended, smiling brightly. "Welcome to the party."

Bowing and feigning confidence, Finch smiled and took Percy's hand in his own. The brigadier's pleasant nature toward lower-ranking officers had made him a target of gossip, but Finch deeply appreciated his kindnesses. "Good evening, sir," he replied, then served himself some punch to ease his nerves.

"That it is, Major," Percy replied, taking a polite dram of punch. "I notice, however, that you are unattended. Where is your wife? How are the children? And your energetic hound? Gus, was it? All well, I presume?"

Finch smiled. "Adelaide fares well, but the children suffer from a bout of cold, and she is at home ministering to their needs. Gus, too, is feeling sorry for himself after he nearly caught a skunk in our garden."

Percy frowned. "Oh dear. I wish them a speedy recovery."

"What a good-hearted fellow. I wonder why he is without an escort, himself."

Finch noticed that Gage, standing a distance off, was at last open to an audience. "Excuse me a moment," Finch said to Percy, putting down his tumbler.

Gathering up his courage, Finch purposefully strode over to where General Gage and his wife Margaret had positioned

3

themselves to welcome their guests. He smiled and screwed up his courage.

"Governor Gage, sir! Your servant!" Finch bowed slightly before him, then kissed Margaret's outstretched hand. "I trust you are well?"

"Well enough," was Gage's stressed reply. His stiff posture and furrowed brow conveyed his no-nonsense personality. "Hardly the time for a birthday celebration, what with all the mess in the colonies." Gage sighed, causing Finch to wonder exactly who had planned and prepared the festivities. "But I suppose everyone needs a rest from the madness of late. I hope you are well, Major...Lynch, yes?"

Finch smiled uncomfortably. "Finch, sir. And I quite agree. The colonies are not by any means content to stand by whilst we celebrate, I fear. I would suggest that while you entertain your guests, it might behoove you to plan for the days ahead."

Gage snorted, pawing the parquet with his foot. "What had you in mind, sir?" The general eyed the small line beginning to form behind Finch. "Speak quickly, Major, for you are not the only man to want for my attention."

Finch took a deep breath and steadied himself.

"May I suggest a diplomatic intervention, Governor Gage? Crown to colony. We must convince them to fulfill their obligation to pay their taxes, while formally hearing their grievances."

Gage glared at him. "Continue."

Finch began to stammer as more onlookers gathered. "W-well, His Majesty spent a significant sum to finance the most recent war with France in order to protect the very colonies that started this war. Now we need their money. I think it best we not rouse the insurgents to arms whilst collecting remuneration from them."

Gage rolled his eyes, but before the governor could speak,

Finch continued. "In these unstable times, we must avoid another armed conflict."

Finch saw that Gage was glaring impatiently at him. He gulped and said. "This will be a challenge, I know. The many taxation acts that have been passed and repealed have caused considerable consternation. You must approach them, sir. Speak your mind to those inclined toward rebellion. Become their friend. Smile. We know you to be a compassionate sort. Your wife is also quite diplomatically inclined, and perhaps even sympathetic to their plight, and—"

"What's that?" Gage thundered.

Now I've done it, Finch thought, beginning to sweat.

Gage had stiffened into a cold rage. In the awkward pause that followed, Finch tried to find a means to mollify the general.

"Sir," Finch said. "There is no shame in feeling sympathy for our colonists. We all feel it is a shame that everyone must pay for the aggression of the Virginian militia that began the Seven Years War. This tax is unfortunate but necessary, and it is well that you uphold it only reluctantly. Shows heart." Finch patted his own chest.

There was another uneasy pause. Finch fiddled with his hat nervously as Gage put his hands on his hips, lips pursed. "So, Major...Pinch?"

Giles sighed. "Finch, si—"

"Yes yes. I knew that. Major Finch. So you want me to show the rebels my softer side. You realize that this approach did not work for poor Governor Hutchinson. I recall that he was your bosom friend prior to my arrival as his replacement."

In Boston, Finch had become fast friends with the intelligent, kindly, and politically ineffectual Thomas Hutchinson. This governor had made himself look weak in multiple ways. First he half-heartedly instated the Stamp Act, levied by Parliament, to help pay for the Seven Years War.

Then he abruptly and gracelessly caved to protesters and appealed to Parliament for the repeal of the law. Meanwhile, rioting Colonials caused the deaths of several men, including a few tax collectors who did their duty without proper security.

"Governor Hutchinson was too sweet from the beginning," Finch said. "He was unwilling to display military might which he did not have to begin with. By contrast, General, you have shown the iron fist; now open your palm and drape it in velvet. The Rebels, knowing that you stand ready to crush them, will realize that you are open to diplomacy as well and that you are kindly disposed toward them. They will surely attend such sentiments with interest."

Gage nodded, a smile crossing his face. Whether it was polite or genuine, Finch could not tell. "I...thank you for your insights, Major. Please enjoy the party, and I will consider this approach. I promise nothing, but I recognize that it is better to attempt to hold the moral high ground than to reduce the countryside to ashes and geld all the males, as suggested by Grant here." He pointed over Finch's shoulder.

Finch flinched and turned. The wrinkled, squint-eyed Scottish colonel of the Fifty-Fifth Foot had snuck up behind him. Grant's yellow-toothed smile, gleaming in the moonlight, was deeply disconcerting.

"As you say, sir," Grant replied to Gage, then turned to Finch. "Gelding is my specialty."

Lexington Green, Lexington, Massachusetts

March 15, 1775, 7:30 AM

Finch looked on as the elderly, rugged Major John Pitcairn cheerfully hallooed the assembled colonial mob. Seated astride a strong chestnut thoroughbred, Pitcairn surveyed the throng with a smile. Then he spurred his mount ahead, escorting Governor General Thomas Gage, also mounted, to meet the Sons of Liberty.

"Right ho, then, chaps," Pitcairn shouted across the green. "We've seen our fair share of conflict already now. We know you're upset. Let's chat a spell, shall we?"

To Finch's great relief, after five days of heated discussion among the various dignitaries of Boston, his suggestion of reconciliation with the Sons of Liberty had been accepted. His military superiors had found it a reasoned approach for ensuring the well-being of all Massachusetts. After some correspondence by mounted messenger with the Sons, this meeting had been arranged. Finch, Pitcairn, and Gage, escorted by two companies of fifty men each, were here to undo the designs of the growing Rebellion by means of diplomacy.

Finch smiled, delighted to at last see a meeting between colony and Crown transpire. He watched as the British soldiers in red coats clasped their hands upon their bayonet-fixed muskets. *Surely their presence would instill the proper amount of respect in the colonials, even as they seemed to undermine our gesture of goodwill,* the veteran engineer thought. Finch then noticed a small, but quickly growing picket of armed Rebels gathering, and he wondered if perhaps such protection was for the best. Even Pitcairn's presence, a surprise to Finch, was not entirely unwelcome, the marine having long been respected by Colonials, on both sides of the political fence, Finch included.

It was a misty morning. The sun was taking its time to rise above the tree line in the distance. The flag of truce held by the ensign of the Sixty-Fifth Foot waved in the breeze alongside the Crown regiment's colors. *Perhaps God may yet smile upon this conference,* Finch thought.

Pitcairn addressed the assembled Sons of Liberty, his Scottish brogue echoing in the clearing. "Gentlemen, I present your governor, Thomas Gage."

There was some polite applause, coupled with stony glares, as the marine helped Gage from his mount. The dapple grey charger, now relieved of his burden, snorted and pawed at the dirt.

Gage modestly waved away the audience's lukewarm response and addressed his opposite – a tall, gangly man who carried himself aristocratically. He wore a powdered wig, a cyan coat, a tricorn hat with a white Jacobite cockade, and an array of tasteful jewelry. Finch was surprised by the number of everyday citizens whose gazes revealed their utmost respect for their well-dressed leader.

"Right. Let us make this quick then," Gage said. "Mister Hancock, your Sons of Liberty have been a damned thorn in my side and in my efforts to keep the peace. Well done, you. But most of the legislation you seem to contest has been repealed. Show some sense, sir. We both love Boston and have the best interests for her populace at heart. Call your villains off, sir. Stop instigating acts of terror in our fair city. Cease your expansion into the lands of the Natives, with whom we have signed treaties of non-aggression. Do this, and we shall release the prisoners we have arrested over the course of this damnable affair. Otherwise, one of these days we shall catch up to you, and our terms will not be nearly so agreeable."

John Hancock stood silently, nose up. He dipped his hand into his waistcoat pocket for a snuffbox – then, noting his company, withdrew the hand. "General, you do us some honor by recognizing us as a group with whom you would deign to meet." His voice was fruity, unctuous. "However, if you have heard of our exploits, you may remember that our demands include the end of all taxation directed at our colonies, unless we are permitted to represent ourselves in Parliament." Hancock glared into the governor's eyes. "We will not rest until our colonies are freed from these tyrannies. Your men have no right to visit such indignities upon us, to oppress us with soldiery and taxes alike. We of the Sons will not relent!"

Gage blinked and shook his head. "So, it is that simple then, eh?"

"Truly," Hancock replied.

Gage pondered this response. He placed his hands on his hips.

"What if we were to reopen Boston Harbor, whose closure you brought upon yourselves with your Tea Party? That way, trade could continue unabated, and we could further ensure that our soldiers, heroes from the war with France, only encamp in your abandoned warehouses and inns for the winter, rather than the entire year 'round? We shall, of course, ship them home as soon as possible. They are of use to neither of us here in the colonies."

Hancock sighed wearily. "Those wars are wars past, sir. By posting soldiers in our taverns and warehouses, you stifle our commerce. And you have harmed only yourselves by closing Boston Harbor in the first place. For it is you who receive the blame for the strangling of the trade that I, as a legitimate merchant, so val—"

"Legitimate merchant?" Gage interrupted.

Finch found himself smiling grimly. Hancock was a known smuggler.

"You, sir," Gage continued, "could easily end the conflict by paying reparations to the East India Company after your so-called Tea Party. As for our soldiery, which would you prefer? To be subject to miniscule, provisional taxes and to play host to some temporary guests to make up for a war you provoked, but we fought on your behalf? Or to rot under French control?"

Hancock shook his head grimly. "Then there is the Quebec Act. We do not wish for an army of Papists and their sympathizers to rule Quebec."

Gage's eyebrows shot up. "And what business is it of yours if one of our protestant governors allows a French-populated colony hundreds of miles away the freedom to worship Jesus in their way, if it keeps them content?" His tone turned sarcastic. "Are you afraid that Governor Carleton will convert, march the Papists southward to Boston, and proselytize to us?"

The two men stared at each other in stony silence.

After a long pause, the governor tugged at his shirt collar, clearly upset, but reining in his emotions. "Well, then," Gage muttered. "I see no need for violence this day. There would be great shame in arresting the lot of you under a flag of truce. It is a terrible tragedy we cannot reach an accord, however."

"Quite," Hancock said, stiffly extending his hand.

Gage regarded it warily, before forcing a smile and gingerly extending both of his own to shake it.

The two factions began to part ways.

Then it happened.

The distinctive *krak* of musketry brought many men on both sides to the dirt.

Finch looked about wildly as Hancock dashed to safety. A small cloud billowed from the Rebel lines as the smell of rotten egg and wood smoke wafted through the air. Finch then looked to the British lines, where he saw Gage lying upon the ground.

Finch charged forward to aid the governor. Unharmed, Gage spluttered with rage and brushed dirt off his waistcoat as Finch helped him to his feet.

"General, are you quite all right, sir?"

"Unhand me!" Gage roughly pushed Finch's hands off of his uniform. "*What the blazes!? We were under a flag of truce!*"

"For pity's sake, sir!" Major Pitcairn shouted from a few feet away, a horrified expression on his face. "It were only one shot. There is no need to war over a single musketball."

"One shot too many, I think," Gage replied, drawing

himself up proudly. "I was assured there would be no exchange of lead on this occasion. Gentlemen! Prime and load!"

The Crown soldiers, caught off guard, fumbled for their firelocks.

Finch sighed, kicking the ground. *If only both sides had thought better than to bring ball and shot to a conference of peace.*

"Make ready!" Gage roared.

Pitcairn stood aghast. "Stand down, lads!" he cried, swatting his hat on the muskets of the closest men.

Finch looked up to see a ragged crowd of musket-wielding Sons of Liberty forming into a line.

"*Give fire!*" came a cry from across the green. A moment later, shots flooded the ranks of the Crown detachment.

As the redcoats around him rushed to ready their muskets, Finch barely heard Gage and Pitcairn shout orders to return fire. He dropped to the ground and began priming his own pistol. *Very well,* he thought. *If it is a fight they truly want, we shall not back down, damn them all.*

The skirmish was sudden and jarring. Both sides seemed unprepared for combat on this field. The Rebel volleys that followed the initial shots were scattered and ineffectual.

The Crown forces fared better. Though they had been caught off guard, the redcoats outnumbered the colonials and were better trained. They kept their order and fired a volley before Pitcairn's voice pierced the smoke. "We've done enough damage, lads!" Pitcairn cried. "Time to control this disaster. *Charge bayonets! Drive them—*"

Krakow!

Pitcairn fell on one knee with an uncharacteristic curse as his leg was dealt a glancing blow. Finch's mouth shot open. The deliberate shooting of an officer of either side in times of war was a hanging offense.

Working his way behind a line of redcoats, Finch struggled over to his friend. But by the time Finch reached Pitcairn, a pair of soldiers had rushed to the marine major's aid and were helping him to the rear.

Meanwhile, the rest of the British line began advancing on the Rebels, who fled with terrified cries of "Every man for himself!"

Finch watched as the Rebels quit the battlefield in disarray. Then he looked about to take stock of the damage.

It had been a small scuffle, with very few injured on either side. Aside from Pitcairn, he saw one redcoat limping along, supported by his friends, and three militiamen lying dead or badly wounded. Finch hoped this diplomatic disaster would be considered nothing more than a small skirmish and would not be inflated into a subject of propaganda, as the incident at King Street – the so-called "Boston Massacre" – had been some five years before.

Gage, however, did not wish for the battle to end so soon. Incensed, he took advantage of Pitcairn's injury. "Avenge our brother in arms, lads!" he cried. "Fire at will!" He drew his saber and flourished it. "Those men were here today to kill us. See to it they do not have another chance! For Pitcairn!"

With a roar, the Crown soldiers charged forward. Gage, fire in his eyes, pulled aside an enlisted man. "Take my horse, lad, and get you to Percy's headquarters at Munroe's Tavern at once! The outcome of this battle depends upon reinforcements. Rouse Pigott, Grant, and Smith to arms. We have them this time!"

Then Gage turned to Finch. "Well, sir, it seems your 'diplomatic approach' did not end as well as we would have liked."

"We tried our best, sir," Finch said. "Do not blame yourself." Inwardly, he kicked himself. He could not believe he had just said something so stupid to his commanding officer. He coughed and managed to stammer, "A-at least by seeking out peace and not firing first, we now have the moral high ground."

Gage frowned. "We shall talk about this later. Return to your duties, Major...Finch." He snapped his fingers. "*Finch.* I shall walk home, whilst you and Pitcairn will wait for Grant and attach this expedition to his larger force. Follow his orders to the letter."

"Yes, sir."

After briefly coughing to get the musket smoke out of his lungs, Finch turned and headed toward the front lines. The Rebels were in full retreat, and it seemed to Finch that their minds were set on nothing but survival.

Pitcairn approached, on his mount once more. "Damned awful sight," the marine remarked sadly.

"Indeed," replied Finch, smoothing his hair nervously. "I feel this is far from over. Shall we call off the men and rest them whilst we wait for Grant and his expedition?"

"Absolutely. We don't want our soldiers fatigued just yet."

Pitcairn looked down the green at his men. "Crown forces!" he shouted. "Break off the pursuit! We will now rest a time!"

For the next 40 minutes, 100 beleaguered soldiers milled about the field, unsure of what was to come. Then, in the distance, came the sounds of fife and drum, coupled with footfalls travelling at a quick march.

Finch turned to see, in the distance, some 200 more men snaking toward the green from town. Reinforcement was on the way.

With mixed feelings, Finch reached inside his coat for his spyglass, then extended it and peered through it. Surveying the troops, he ascertained that about 100 of these men were soldiers of the light infantry companies belonging to the Sixty-Fifth and Eighteenth Foot; the other 100 or so were their grenadier company counterparts. To the tune of the quick and upbeat "March of the British Grenadiers," their columns made their way forward.

Leading these men, trotting on horseback, were Colonels Robert Pigott and Francis Smith, with Grant in supreme command. All three sat at ease in the saddle, as though off on a casual summer's ride.

Grant rode straight up to Pitcairn and Finch.

"Major?" Grant said, smiling at Pitcairn and disregarding Finch. "I am taking command of this expedition. I heard there was some difficulty in the…diplomatic proceedings. Now that we have come to blows, I welcome you to assist me in quashing this insurgency. We must find the depot that supplied these ingrates."

Concord, Massachusetts

March 15, 1775, 10:47 AM

After caucusing with his officers, Grant ordered the detachment to march to Concord. Along the way, they flushed a few wayward Sons of Liberty from trees and brush.

Now the Crown soldiers stood in the small town, squinting under the brightly shining sun in their itchy woolen coats, awaiting orders.

"You there, Captain!" hissed Colonel Grant to Captain Byrd, who stood a few feet away. "Take your company and search the town!"

"At once, sir!" Byrd piped, saluting. He turned to his light infantry company and said with surprising joviality, "Well, lads! That's our cue! Split into groups of two and go house to house. McMillan's and Smith's platoons from the west, Elway's and Atkinson's from the east. Engage the locals with a certain civility, if you please."

Even as they fanned out in search of arms and powder, however, it was clear to Finch that the expedition was showing signs of fatigue and frustration. Many of the less experienced soldiers had become nervous. They were not accustomed to this sort of resistance. This was nothing like the past powder alarms they had endured. By now, too, all the men were exhausted and in no mood to be courteous. As they searched, they roughly shoved citizens aside. The colonists grumbled and cursed as they gave way to British numbers and steel. "Go back to England, damned lobsterbacks!" cried a passing young boy. A moment later, he heaved a rock in the direction of the soldiers.

One redcoat deflected it with his musket instinctively, and made to break formation with his platoon. "Steady, Mulroy," his sergeant told him. "No sense in riling up the locals further. We've a long day ahead of us." The soldier nodded.

Finch followed Grant and several soldiers as they inspected the town's dwellings. When no ammunition turned up after an hour's search, Grant began to get restless. Worrying for the safety of the townsfolk as Grant's mood soured, Finch picked out two soldiers from the group he was tailing and set off with them to make some random searches of his own.

A few minutes later, just as Grant appeared around a street corner, Finch noticed a suspicious-looking storage building behind a small house. "All right," he said to his men. "Have a look." The soldiers approached the building, with Finch and Grant following closely behind. They creaked the door open to reveal two dozen muskets and a small supply of powder and ammunition. It was a modest supply, but enough to arm a resistance cell.

Grant let loose with a string of curses. Then he shot Finch a smile of pure venom. "Major? The charges, if you please. Let us blow this cache sky high. These so-called 'civilians' have misled us, stolen our gunpowder, and fired upon us with glee.

Let us punish them for their transgressions against the Crown. Concord must burn!"

"No!" a voice cried.

Finch turned. A small group of colonials had gathered around them. The call had come from a pockmarked, well-dressed man who looked on in wide-eyed terror.

"You cannot do this!" bleated a middle-aged woman in a blue dress, wringing her hands in concern.

"Sir," intoned a large black man, reaching out calmly toward the Crown soldiers. "Many of us are loyal to the Crown. Your actions against the insurgency have given us hope. I do believe that with your help and guidance, we can now hold against their foul design."

"Aye, hold just one minute, lads, let's not be rash!" another citizen shouted. He rushed toward the soldiers, who immediately levelled their muskets at him. He stopped, gulped, and hastily retreated a few steps. "With the presence of your manpower and your guidance, the scum don't stand a chance!"

"Think of the children!" cried an elderly preacher, flailing his arms. "God clearly smiles upon your efforts! You have come so far! Do not let the children be corrupted by the rebellion's propaganda."

Grant stepped next to Finch and looked straight into the preacher's eyes. "I regret to say that I am not sorry, Reverend." He reached for his pistol. Priming it, he said, "We cannot spare the manpower to hold this strategically insignificant position. You are welcome back in Boston, but we can offer no further assistance here at this time. Finch?"

Finch snapped to attention and stepped forward. "Here, sir."

Grant smiled darkly. "We're waiting. Blow up this storehouse. We will then set the town alight."

Finch frowned. "Sir, what you are suggesting would

undoubtedly be seen as a great atrocity. If we set fire to the town, we will place the Crown in a world of trouble with respect to colonial relations. The fate of Concord will be held against us for decades, even if a revolution is circumvented, and—"

Grant snorted, eyes aglow. "Damn the diplomacy, sah! The Rebels had their chance to pursue their grievances diplomatically. Then, when they chose to fight us, they injured an officer! It is time to take drastic measures! If you will not torch this village, Major, then I shall."

Grant grabbed the nearest soldier and pulled him close. "Retrieve one of the powder kegs from within."

"Yes, sir," the soldier said. He hurried away.

The preacher spoke up again. "This will accomplish nothing! Take the powder and weapons with you. Use them in your fight against the Rebels. Surely there is no need to cause such wanton destruction."

"I care not for such details," Grant hissed. He paused and thought for a moment. "Very well, Reverend. I shall spare this miserable town from the ashes. Still, these illegal weapons will be destroyed."

Soon the soldier returned, cradling the keg of powder in his arms. He set it gently on the ground. Grant forced out its stopper, then slowly spread a line of powder from where he stood to the inside of the outbuilding. Through the open door, Finch watched him spread the remainder of the powder on and around the weapons.

Grant reemerged from the shed, wiping his hands free of powder. He strode confidently back to the gathered soldiers.

"Now, Major, would you kindly lead these civilians away to a safe distance? I would hate for someone to be injured," Grant ordered, his voice scathing.

Finch nodded. "Yes, Colonel." He turned to face the crowd. "You heard Colonel Grant! Let us away from here.

17

Men, assist the townsfolk to safety, behind the stone wall there, across the field."

Clearly disheartened, the soldiers nonetheless did their duty and began herding the citizens away.

"Sir! You mustn't!" an aging woman pleaded. But she did not resist the soldier pulling her arms.

"I say nay!" a young man suddenly shouted. He broke from the crowd, ducked under the grasping arms of the soldiers, and sprinted toward Grant.

In one swift motion, Grant brought his pistol to bear upon the man. As Finch looked on in horror, Grant fired one shot. The young man's body crumpled to the ground, his legs still briefly pumping.

Finch heard the strangled gasps and cries of the townsfolk. Despite his revulsion, he knew that the worst thing to do now would be to show weakness. He stood tall as he gestured to the soldiers to continue following their orders.

As soon as the townsfolk were safely away, Colonel Grant used the spark from his pistol's flint to ignite the powder trail. Then he beat a hasty retreat.

The powder burned along the ground and into the shed. A moment later, the shed erupted into bright flames that billowed out the open door. Then the remaining powder ignited, and the entire shed exploded with a great roar. Everyone, Colonel Grant included, ducked to avoid the flying debris.

Finch stood back up and looked grimly upon the stunned colonists. Somehow, in the past few minutes, they had greatly swollen in numbers.

"Fool," said the preacher softly, his arms stiff at his sides.

Grant's jaw was set, his eyes bright with confidence. "I have upheld justice and the King's law," he announced, crossing his arms and glaring at the crowd.

The preacher glanced at the dead boy's body, then at the

burning barn, then at Grant. "May God spit on you and your offspring, all of you."

The comment bit through Finch's resolve, and he grimaced. Grant simply shrugged and fell back into formation. He addressed his soldiers. "Gentlemen, our work here is all but finished. Let us give the town one or two more thorough sweeps. I have grown suspicious after this encounter." He turned to the townsfolk. "As Crown soldiers, it is also our duty to see those of Loyal proclivities to Boston and safety. Does anyone wish to join us?"

A terrified few stepped forward. There were mutinous mutterings among those who did not.

Grant looked down his nose and sniffed haughtily. "Very well, then. You will attend nearby as we search for more supplies belonging to the enemy here and across the Concord River. When we finish, we shall escort you to safety in Boston."

The Old North Bridge, Concord, Massachusetts

March 15, 1775, 12:27 PM

Finch and his men had spent the past hour performing a few additional sweeps of the town's outskirts. Grant had said that he did not want to miss any additional hidden caches of weaponry, but Finch suspected that he delighted in tormenting the town's citizens.

Eventually, Grant announced to his soldiers, "Our inspection here is complete. There do not seem to be any further supplies on this side of the Concord River. We shall now cross this bridge and continue the search. There are a few more farms that look especially suspicious." He smiled.

The Crown soldiers grumbled softly. Inwardly, so did Finch. It had been a long and gut-wrenching day, and Finch, like his men, were beginning to doubt Grant's motives – and perhaps his mental stability.

As Finch, Pitcairn, and their men approached the bridge, Finch noticed a flicker of movement behind some brush. He dove for cover just in time.

A sudden volley flew high over the heads of the redcoats. Armed farmers jumped out from behind the brush, then began clumsily converging into a column. They slowly made their way across the Old North Bridge, which led to a dirt track through a broad meadow. Once they were on the opposite side of the river, they wheeled about, intent on making a stand at this new position.

Finch cursed, clenching his fists. He turned to Pitcairn. "Ambushed *again!* And it seems the rustics are well positioned this time. If we charge across, we'll be bottlenecked."

Pitcairn smiled sorrowfully at Finch. "But if we get across, our grenadiers will make short work of them. Will you shepherd the men into position, Major Finch? I need to take a piss."

Finch gathered his wits and began to issue orders. "Captain Perkins!" he cried, cupping his hands around his mouth.

Perkins, a gruff but talented veteran promoted from the ranks in the Seven Years War, sprang to attention. Finch gave him an appraising look and noticed that his right forefinger was heavily bandaged – a new wound from earlier in the day.

"Sah?" Perkins replied.

"Maneuver your men in front of this bridge. Have some of them drop their packs and erect a small barricade, whilst the rest exchange shots with the enemy. If the Rebels block our path on the other side, we shall blast our way through with superior firepower from behind cover."

"Sah!" Perkins said again. He turned and roared orders to his sergeants, who in turn bellowed their commands to their enlisted men. Some of the men shrugged off their sturdy goatskin packs and began stacking them to create a barrier.

A Rebel volley suddenly crackled past Finch. He cried out in surprise as a musketball embedded itself in his coat. He clutched at the coat and scanned his body for injury. There was none. He eased the ball from his jacket and took a knee to regain his composure.

A small band of redcoats ran to his aid, but he waved them away. "What are you waiting for, lads?" he cried. "Help them fortify our side of the bridge!"

The soldiers turned and hurried to the front. As musketballs flew past them, they took off their backpacks and stacked them atop or alongside those of their fellow redcoats. They then took positions behind the barrier, kneeling to load and standing only to fire over the shoulders of their comrades.

Meanwhile, Colonels Pigott and Smith led their reinforcements to the front at a quick march, each commander tipping his hat in turn to Finch as they neared. Smith smiled confidently. "Well done, Finch. You've got their dander up! While the hat companies engage their front, we will prepare the men in a battle line behind them. Then, on the word, we'll charge with the bayonet across the bridge en masse and overrun their position."

"Very well," Finch replied, saddened at the thought of the bloodshed to come. "Though I suggest that if we can also flank their position, they shall be in a sorry state indeed."

Smith nodded dismissively. "Aye, but it will not drill home our victory the same way. I shall conduct the action from that ridge over yonder." He pointed not far off before returning his gaze to the engineer. "Ready the men, Mister Finch."

Finch organized the steady stream of men into a position perpendicular to the bridge, about 20 feet back from the riverbank, behind the barricade. Amidst the smell of powder and the sounds of musketry, Rebels and redcoats glared at each other, each daring the other to attempt a crossing.

The Rebel force's numbers were swelling quickly. The locals, hearing the clash of arms, had equipped themselves, and were hurrying toward the bridge, taking up positions.

Finch was not content to see men die on his watch without rendering what assistance he could. He strode quickly to the front, flinching as powder exploded all around him. Musketballs skipped past and smoke enshrouded him.

He ducked behind the barricade, drew his spyglass from his coat, and surveyed the scene. Crown soldiers, lips black from powder, blasted volley after volley at the enemy. The fields before him were littered with the injured and dying, yet it was difficult to count the fallen because of the obscuring smoke. *The butcher's bill is being paid today*, Finch thought as he surveyed the carnage.

A sergeant standing near Finch rallied his men. "Alright, lads. We are going to spring up from behind this barricade and fire off a volley, then take cover, reload, rise up, and volley again. We must keep up our fire until we clear them out or are given the order to charge. They will show no mercy if we give pause. Are we all loaded up?"

"Yes, sir!" came a practiced, chorused reply.

"Make ready!"

Click went several locks near Finch.

"Present!"

Suddenly, two redcoats went down as a pair of Rebel sharpshooters found their marks. There was a moment's silence.

"Give fire! Now, boys! Pour it into them!"

A loud volley crackled away at the Rebel forces. Finch heard howls of pain from the far side of the bridge.

Once again, Finch lifted his spyglass and surveyed the territory on all sides. For a moment, some of the smoke of battle cleared. Finch spotted, far to the south, about half a mile away, a small, secondary bridge spanning the Concord River. There appeared to be no sign of enemy presence nearby.

Opportunity.

I have to inform high command about this bridge. Finch clambered to his feet, then ran toward the ridge from which Smith, mounted on his warhorse, was directing the battle.

A powerful volley went off from the British lines. For one moment, Finch stopped and looked back. Three thin red lines – one kneeling, one crouching, one standing – were engulfed in smoke. He turned to see the Rebel line reel, like a snake aflame.

Finch gathered his wits. With his head down and his hands over his ears, he made his way at a brisk pace toward Colonel Smith.

But when Finch reached the corpulent, baby-faced Colonel two minutes later, Smith was no longer on his horse. He had been shot and was sitting on the ground, bleeding profusely, being attended to by two grenadiers. Both had very grim looks upon their faces.

"Colonel Smith!" Finch shouted. "Can you hear me?"

Smith moaned softly, clutching a gaping musketball wound in his chest. The shot had left much gore in its wake.

"Request permission to lead the lights across an unguarded bridge just south of here," Finch said quickly. "With luck, I feel we could take their flank."

An angry voice bellowed behind Finch. "Damn your eyes, Major! Stand off! Can you not see the man is injured?"

Finch swung around. Colonel Grant, mounted on his horse, scowled at him. "Now, what is it you want?"

"Sir, the enemy has neglected to guard a bridge about a half mile to the south. I was hoping to guide the lights over the crossing and strike the enemy's exposed flank."

The colonel's lips pursed. He thrust out his hand for

Finch's spyglass. "Let's have a look, then. Brigadier General Percy sends his compliments. He has artillery standing by at Munroe's Tavern, ready to offer support at our request."

Finch nodded and wordlessly handed over the spyglass. Grant took it and peered through it in the direction of the south bridge. He grinned.

"Good job, Finch." He handed back the spyglass. "Take the light bobs under Pigott across the river at once. I shall supervise Pitcairn and the rest of the lads here. Keep your distance from the scum on the other side of this bridge; they are bringing in reinforcements, so I shall clear them away with a barrage. When it concludes, the men will be under orders to advance."

The South Bridge, Concord, Massachusetts
March 15, 1775, 2:45 PM

"So, you're to run with us, eh, Finch?" Pigott inquired, dismounting from his horse to lead the light infantry battalion on foot.

"Yes, sir. Grant's orders," Finch replied, straightening his hat. "I found another bridge, this one to the south and left completely unguarded, spanning the Concord River. We are under orders from Grant to cross it and hit the rustics from the flank."

"Splendid!" Pigott replied. He gestured for Finch's spyglass.

Finch handed over the instrument, then guided Pigott's sight to where the bridge stood.

"A very fine catch indeed!" Pigott cried. He collapsed the scope and returned it to Finch. Then he turned to his assembled men, two companies of light infantry. He shouted,

"Let us go, lads! Captains? Facilitate this advance! Finch? Try to keep up!"

"You heard the colonel," one of the captains shouted. "Let's go!"

It was an exhausting run to the bridge. The lights were fleet of foot and didn't have much equipment to slow them down. Finch was hard pressed to keep pace with them as they hurried along the banks of the Concord. Huffing and puffing, he was dead last to arrive at the bridge, reaching it just as Pigott ordered a cautious advance across the river.

Pigott smiled kindly at Finch, who was bent over, gasping for breath. He swept a hand toward his men. "All yours, Major Finch," he wheezed good naturedly.

Finch nodded, stood up, took out his spyglass, and surveyed the battle. Once again, he had underestimated the enemy. The colonial force had grown significantly, and now it outnumbered the British force by at least three to one. Men were falling in droves on the Rebel side, but the Crown forces were slowly being whittled down as well.

Pigott turned to Finch. "I thought we'd have artillery. Did Grant mention that to you, perchance?"

Finch frowned. General Percy would not intentionally leave his allies without fire support. "He did," Finch replied, "but something must be very wrong to keep Percy from doing his duty."

"Grant will not last much longer, Finch! What do we do?"

Finch sighed. "We attack. If we get caught in a cannonade, so be it!"

Finch ordered the men forward through the woods – slowly, and as quietly as possible.

After ten minutes, they were no more than two hundred feet from the Rebels' flank, and largely out of their view.

Wiping away beads of sweat, Finch gestured the men forward with a few waves of his hand, pointing to various vantage points. "Get into position, lads. We must not be seen by the enemy. Our victory lies in surprise."

To Finch's chagrin, then relief, the lights looked to Pigott for guidance. He nodded them onward. "This is Finch's expedition, lads. I'm just here to oversee the operation. Mark him well."

Musketry echoed in the distance, distracting the Rebel forces and covering the Crown advance.

"Right, lads!" Finch cried loudly, before remembering that he was attempting to spring an ambush and lowering his voice. "Up! And to your posts."

The lights sprang up and began to take action, but halted, grumbling slightly as Finch proceeded to offer more instructions. "Position yourselves along the tree line and pour it on. They cannot hit what they cannot see. Just remember to be sure to fire in volleys. We need to frighten the bastards away from our main force. Now prime and load! *COURAGE!*"

The lights flew into position. Crouched amongst the trees, the Crown soldiers crept ever closer to their quarry.

"Make ready!" Finch rasped to the soldiers around him. They raised their muskets and clicked their locks into place. Others, noting their activity, followed suit.

"Present!"

The muskets were levelled.

To his horror, Finch saw in the distance that a colonial fighter had noticed their position. Wide-eyed, the minuteman was frantically attempting to get the attention of his commander, tapping him on the shoulder and pointing toward the woods.

"Give fire! Prime and load!"

The lights made their muskets heard, their volleys resounding through the forest.

The Rebel line wavered as it was suddenly pressed by heavy fire from two sides. Grant's men, sensing weakness, began to move into a position to charge.

Finch held up his spyglass and peered through it. Across the river, the regulars were cheering the appearance of the lights, and Grant was waving his hat in Finch's direction. As the lights continued to skirmish from Finch's position in the woods, Finch looked on in horror as Grant formed up his grenadiers and, in a voice inaudible half a mile off, ordered a charge.

"NO, dammit!" Finch hissed to himself. "You're leading them into a bottleneck!" Turning to Pigott, Finch cried, "We've got to save them!"

Pigott nodded. "You've done well, Finch, but it is time for an old veteran to retake command." He cleared his throat, then roared, "Light infantry! *Follow me!*"

The lights leapt out of the woods and thrust with their bayonets into the flank of the surprised militia, slowly breaking the Rebel line from the side. But the enemy, in turn, rocked the entrapped British forces crossing the bridge with heavy musketry. Men fell on both sides of the river, their cries echoing across the fields.

Despite his pudgy physique, Pigott fought like the devil, thrusting and slashing with his hanger blade. Watching him, Finch counted five Rebels laid low before him as he fought from the front.

A moment later, Finch's heart clutched in horror as a Rebel took aim and fired, his shot catching Pigott in the throat. The colonel fell to his knees, gurgling for breath.

Meanwhile, the grenadiers poured over and around the makeshift goatskin barricade and charged across the bridge – straight into a wall of flesh-rending lead. They fell several at a time, creating a mass of tangled bodies.

At long last, like an avenging angel, Pitcairn appeared, dodging and weaving and thrusting and slashing with his blade amid the front lines of his regulars. "Onward, men!

Rally upon me and break them, lads!" He grimly advanced as he gritted his teeth in pain from his earlier wounds.

His men came to the aid of the grenadier battalion, which now numbered about 60. They, too, pushed their attack forward with renewed vigor, their faces knit with determination beneath their bearskin caps.

The militia was not broken yet, however. As the Crown forces loomed closer, they fired yet another volley, dropping several more men.

Although the British soldiers fell in great numbers, the reinforcement of the grenadiers by the regulars was too much for the Rebels. The militia began to fall back, firing as they withdrew. With their line broken, their individual shots proved largely ineffectual. Soon, the rustics were all but driven from the field. Many dropped their fowlers and ran full tilt for home.

Finch looked on as his lights whooped for joy. One soldier sounded a hunting horn, and the redcoats chased after some of the retreating rebels. Soon, a dozen or so minutemen were overtaken by the invigorated light bobs, who roughed them up, searched them, and began assembling them into a line of prisoners.

Grant had now ridden to the front, his face red from the exertion. He smiled as his men thumped the heads and twisted the arms of their captives behind their backs, restraining them as they were searched for hidden weaponry. After viewing the brutality to his satisfaction, he turned to Finch and extended his hand.

"We've done well, Finch. What a fine body of fellows you commanded. And see how the enemy runs! We've given the bastards what for!"

Finch shrugged, gasping for air as he tugged at his constricting horsehair neckstock. He sighed, looking at the many dozens of fallen men, hardly believing this could be called a victory. "I did my best. There are many men of ours amongst the dead as a result of my actions."

"And many more dead pissants," Grant replied. "Come, let us press them further still!"

Grant turned to address his troops, who were milling around, some looting the dead. Before he could speak, however, a loud crack echoed through the woods. Both Grant and Finch turned instinctively.

"Those are rifles!" Pitcairn cried, brandishing his saber. "Quick, lads! Whilst they reload! One last charge! We are nearly—"

Krak!

Grant, struck, fell to his knees, cursing a bullet that had embedded itself in his shoulder. Finch rushed to his side, but was quickly waved away by Pitcairn. Colonel Grant clambered to his feet, shaking in rage.

"Cowards!" Grant bellowed. He strode imperiously toward the ensign of the Sixty-Fifth Foot, who cringed at the sight of the imposing Scotsman. Grant ripped the standard from the ensign's arms and turned to Captain O'Donnell, who stood beside him. "Intersperse these half-wits amongst the trees! Find the riflemen!"

O'Donnell flinched before saluting. "At once, sir!"

As the Crown forces moved out, bayonets glinting in the sun, a ragged, haggard band of rifle-wielding men broke from cover at the edge of the woods.

"Stand down, riflemen!" Grant shouted. "Your war is over!"

"Liberty!" one of the Rebels cried in defiance. His shout was echoed by the others. Then, as one, they turned and made for home as quickly as their legs could carry them.

"Shoot them! Shoot them!" Grant bellowed.

Finch fumbled for his pistol and began to prime and load

it. Around him, dozens of other Crown soldiers did the same. But the last of the Rebels quickly melted away.

"Our sally is now complete," Grant snarled. He shifted his focus to Finch. "We have won the day. Let us mount up and return to Boston."

Finch couldn't help himself. Stepping out of formation, he asked, "Sir, should we not report to Brigadier General Percy's headquarters, and determine why his artillery did not join us?"

Grant pondered a moment. "Very well," he said crossly. "Let us investigate." He then turned to Perkins, the scarred Seven Years War veteran. "Captain Perkins?"

Perkins hurried forward. "Sah?" he rasped, scratching his nose.

Grant gestured idly to the mass of Concord Loyalists milling about behind the redcoats. "I will lead a small detachment of your men and escort these misbegotten refugees to Boston." He turned to Finch. "The rest of you, eyes peeled. You're off to Munroe's."

Munroe's Tavern, Lexington, Massachusetts
March 15, 1775, 4:07 PM

"Fire, sir! In the tavern!"

Finch stepped out of the column that had been marching toward Munroe's Tavern for the past hour. He saw Captain O'Donnell running toward him, waving his arm. He looked up in horror at the gouts of smoke billowing in the far distance.

"Can you see anything through that smoke, Finch?" inquired Pitcairn, who had also left the column and sat atop his horse, staring down at the two men.

Finch once again took out his spyglass, held it up, and peered through it. He could make out a battery of guns –

recently spiked and rendered useless. On the ground around them were a few redcoats and a scattering of soldiers wearing blue coats with red facings – British fusiliers and their artillerist counterparts. Lying lifeless around them were corpses in civilian attire, clearly Rebel militia. In all, there appeared to be at least 90 dead. A force of Rebels had apparently attacked Percy's command post. There had been a battle, and the Rebels had burnt the tavern to the ground.

"Damnation," Finch murmured, collapsing his glass. "If we lost Percy..." He turned to Pitcairn. "The tavern is in ashes. There was a skirmish. I saw nearly 100 dead. No one alive."

"Blast," Pitcairn muttered. He turned and galloped ahead. O'Donnell followed not far behind. Finch broke into a run toward the ruin.

Finch shook the possibility of Percy's death from his mind. He broke into a run toward the ruin.

A few minutes later, Finch arrived at the remnants of the tavern, now a charred husk. He slowly maneuvered among the casualties littering the grounds.

A glint of polished metal caught Finch's eye. He pushed aside some of the smoldering wreckage with his foot and then, wrapping his hand in a handkerchief, lifted a handsome blade from the hand of a body burnt beyond recognition. Finch noted the ornateness of the blade, however, and knew at once that the body was that of General Percy.

Too late.

Finch found O'Donnell. "Captain?" he said sorrowfully, "General Percy is dead. We have a long march to Boston."

Finch heard hoofbeats rapidly approaching from behind him. He turned to look and saw Pitcairn riding toward him. As he drew closer, Finch could see the tension on his face.

"Sir! We must return to the front at once. We are under heavy fire! We need every soldier we have!"

Finch took one last sympathetic look at Percy before gesturing to the lights to follow him. Then he ran, full tilt, down the stone-paved path.

Pitcairn rode ahead, then began orchestrating a frenzied defense against what seemed to be the advance of a fresh force of Rebel militia.

Finch knew that the more officers who were on the field to supervise the troops, the more at ease they would feel. He turned to the men, raising his voice with the greatest urgency. "Alright lads, look sharp! Deploy at once behind any low stone walls along the path. We're going to need all the cover we can get."

The men, surprised at being ordered about by an engineer but nevertheless obedient, sprang into action. They took up positions behind the walls, murmuring nervously among themselves.

Finch then walked behind them, doing his best to offer encouragement. Making his voice as low as he could, Finch sauntered among the line infantry, occasionally swatting a man on the back. "Worry not, my fine lads. This battle is ours. We shall quash this rebellion, and we shall not die doing it. Why not, you may ask? Because we are so very pretty! Look at us, our chiseled jaws, our scarlet coats! We are too damned beautiful for God to let us die!"

The soldiers looked back at him as though he had gone insane. *At least I amused them a bit*, Finch thought.

Then an imposing force of Rebel fighters began to appear over the crest of a low hill, bearing hatchets, fowlers, and rifles. First came a dozen. Then, as the Crown forces roused themselves to arms, the Rebel numbers grew – first to 50, then to 100. Within a few minutes, a mob of over 800 men at arms stood before them. Finch's stomach plummeted as the front ranks smartly formed into a skirmish line and began to advance on the British position. Behind them was a more substantial battle line formation.

Though the Crown soldiers were able to topple the skirmishers with relative ease, every enemy soldier who fell bought time for the larger force to advance. It did not help that the skirmishers were equipped with rifles, which were far more accurate than muskets. Though these soldiers numbered only a few dozen, with almost every shot they fired, a redcoat soldier fell.

Finch watched as the British took cover, loaded, then stood to fire, before taking cover again to load once more. It occurred to him that perhaps the Rebel militia had stealthily followed his men all this time. Cries of "down with Parliament!" and "a pox on taxation!" filled the air.

Soon both sides had taken up a rhythm of firing, loading, and firing again. But the Rebel forces were slowly advancing between shots, and the redcoats, outnumbered and pinned down, began to fall at a worrisome rate.

Finch lay on his belly behind a low stone wall. He spotted Pitcairn on his horse, about 30 feet away.

"Where did these bastards come from?" he shouted at Pitcairn over the roar of musketry, knowing that Pitcairn could not possibly hear him.

Yet, a moment later, Pitcairn spotted him and frantically waved him over.

Finch slowly clambered to his feet in between volleys and dashed behind some brush. Pitcairn reined in his horse behind a slightly taller section of the wall. It was precious little cover for a man on horseback, but it was all they had. Finch met up with him there.

Pitcairn took Finch's hand in his own, speaking in a low, grim tone. "My dear Giles. I do believe this will be the end of me. We're pinned down and under fire from the front and from the left flank. Our ability to return to Boston has been severed." He quickly surveyed the battlefield. "This will be quite a fight, my dear fellow, and I want you to be safe, so stay well away from me. These men seem to have a penchant for shooting officers."

Finch smiled grimly. "John, I promise you. We shall live to fight another day. We need only make it back to Boston. We shall try our best, and if I die, I can think of precious few people I'd rather die alongside."

"But how can we possibly make it back to Boston?"

Finch looked Pitcairn in the eye. "Charge them, John. We'll break through their lines and run for Boston. It is our one chance. We have a heavily hit, exhausted force, greatly worn down in numbers. How can we defeat this many militiamen? There is no shame in retreating from so dire a situation."

"Retreat?" whispered Pitcairn softly. "In the face of militia? I...I suppose..." He turned to survey the situation. A moment later, volley fire swept in from the Crown's right flank. After a few deep breaths, Pitcairn recovered his composure. "I...it is necessary."

Finch nodded. "Give Captain Byrd the entire light infantry battalion. I shall supervise him. The remnants of the grenadiers, coupled with the hat companies, could breach the enemy lines. We might be able to run through that breach toward Boston. The light bobs would be the last to push through. They could put up a stout, mobile resistance, withdrawing while firing. You can then bring your men to safety and report back a pyrrhic victory, rather than an outright disaster."

Pitcairn's expression was resigned. He massaged his bewigged temples. "As you say, Giles. Let us perform the impossible." He sighed. "Try not to die."

Finch chuckled grimly. "You, too."

Pitcairn sat tall in the saddle and unsheathed his hanger. He gestured to Finch, implying he should have the honor of the final word. Finch coughed nervously. If this failed, the blame would be placed squarely on him.

"Charge your...bayonets!" Finch roared, surprised at the sound of his own voice.

The drums sounded, the fifes trilled, and the Crown expedition sallied from behind the walls.

As the redcoats advanced, three lines of Rebels spouted three volleys of lead from three separate flanks.

Pitcairn flourished his blade, ordering a quick march. "Onward, men! March!...March! March!"

The lights, line, and grenadier infantry quickened to a full run. Chests heaving, lungs gasping for air, the tattered remnants of the Crown's heavy infantry and the colonial militiamen began to converge.

The Rebels started to waver, terror and surprise on their faces. They fired off one more ragged volley, then gave way, leaving a path open for the men of the Crown.

"Move it, lads! *Go!*" Pitcairn cried, beckoning his towering grenadiers and their line infantry counterparts forward. "They will reform soon!"

A few Rebel militiamen recovered their nerve and attempted to plug the gap. Each one received a musket butt to the face or a bayonet to the gut from a Crown soldier. The first contingent of the British forces began moving through the hole in the Rebel lines.

Finch and the light companies continued their own march forward. "Sound the horns, lads!" Finch cried. "That will shake the enemy up some!"

A hunting horn resounded throughout the ranks. "*King George!*" Byrd cried. "*For his Majesty!*" Finch replied.

Though they seemed to not give the enemy much pause, these cries strengthened the resolve of Finch and his men. Their pace quickened, and the battalion advanced with vigor.

The militia's musketry gusted from all sides. Redcoats

fell in droves with cries of agony, calling out for their family and friends. Finch looked around this carnage and noticed the enemy closing in, looking to take the lights captive.

"Volley fire, lads!" Finch cried as he continued to huff and puff forward. "Right up close! They are but one single line of men on each flank. We shall blast our way to freedom!"

His command was followed by a quick, efficient volley of musketry from the light bobs. The shots sent many Rebels sprawling to the ground, shrieking in agony.

"*Onward, lads! Now!*" Finch shouted. He led his battalion forward, ever closer to the breach in the Rebel lines.

With a great roar, the Rebels tried once more to close ranks and entrap them. Finch drew his blade and prepared for melee combat. Around him, his allies, equipped with sabers, bayonet-fixed muskets, and hatchets, also prepared to defend themselves.

A pair of Rebels, each seemingly no older than 20, threw themselves at Finch. Fearing for his life, he stepped to one side and pivoted. One Rebel soldier telegraphed his downward chop with a dagger a bit too clearly, and Finch cleaved off his hand with his saber. Finch then pivoted again and parried a blow from his second antagonist. He parried another slash and landed a superficial shoulder injury of his own, cutting through the minuteman's waistcoat and biting lightly into his flesh. Doffing his hat, Finch attempted to end the conflict quickly by suddenly lunging home to dispatch the enemy.

The Rebel saw the lunge coming and twisted out of the way, just in time. Finch stumbled past him. A moment later, the Son of Liberty grabbed Finch's shoulders and forcibly turned him around, smiling malevolently. The young man threw himself on top of Finch, and the two fell to the ground. The Rebel drew his dagger and put it to Finch's throat. Finch closed his eyes and prayed silently for a quick death.

Finch felt the rancid, heavy breathing of the Rebel soldier

on his neck. But the final blow failed to come. Instead, Finch heard a dull thunk.

Finch opened his eyes to see Captain Byrd standing above him, extending a hand to help him up. Beside him, the young Rebel soldier lay dead or unconscious.

"Your servant, Major Finch. I do believe it is time we quit the field."

Finch nodded and stood up. Together, he and Byrd took to their heels after the Crown light infantry, who had surged forward and again broken the Rebel line. They sprinted through as though the hounds of Hell were on their heels. Musketballs tore after them, whistling through the air around them. Beside them, some 100 British soldiers ran with the same urgency and terror.

After making some distance, Finch turned to find the enemy in only casual pursuit. Perhaps a dozen militiamen were ambling after them, firing in their direction. This surprised and even rankled him a bit. Did they no longer consider the redcoats a threat?

Finch slowed to a trot and called out to Byrd. "Captain! Deploy your remaining sharpshooters in teams of two behind cover. We will enact a fighting withdrawal!"

Byrd nodded. "Alright, lads! To the right, about...face!" he piped in his youthful voice. "Break off in teams and take cover!"

Snapping to, the lights quickly peeled off in pairs and sought protection behind trees and walls, or simply by lying prone. Each team took turns firing, then retiring toward the next location offering cover.

Finch pulled out his spyglass and surveyed their surroundings. The Rebel citizen-soldiers had reassembled and were advancing toward them in force once more. "Byrd!" he cried. "Mind the left flank! The enemy approaches!"

"We see them, Major, thank you!" Byrd replied. He

directed his sharpshooters to target the approaching Rebel line. "Take your shots, gentlemen!"

Krak! Krak! Krak! Kaarak! The lights replied, their muskets singing one at a time, toppling over enemy soldiers as they advanced. Two Rebel militiamen fell, then three more, then a group of half a dozen. "That's some damn fine skirmishing!" Finch shouted. "Well done, men!"

Byrd smiled nervously. "Like playing ninepins on a weekend, sir. Though as we have kicked the hornet's nest, it may be best that we go on our way." He turned to his men. "Eyes on the right flank, boys. They're now probing our right! Fall back!"

And so it went, with the Rebels who approached attempting to encircle the British light bobs, who managed to just slip past the enveloping action with minimal casualties. As they began to fall back, they delivered a limited beating of their own, dashing amongst the buildings of Menotomy, whose winding roads forced the Rebels into a march column, and thus made it harder for them to bring their numbers to bear. Finch observed the distraction they wrought through his spyglass then clapped the young captain on the back. "Well done, Byrd! You've given them a bloody nose!"

As they continued their chase of the light infantry, the Rebel casualties mounted. After ten more minutes of cat and mouse, more than 60 dead colonials lay on the path.

As this skirmish wore on, an exasperated-looking militia commander in an expensive violet waistcoat barked an order to his soldiers. His words were inaudible to Finch, but a few seconds later, the exhausted minutemen stopped firing. They shouldered their weapons, then turned and plodded back in the direction of Munroe's Tavern.

"Major Finch," Byrd said. "Recommend we withdraw. We have lost many soldiers from our earlier encounters and should report to General Gage."

Finch nodded. "Let us to our headquarters in Boston."

Governor Thomas Gage's Mansion, Boston, Massachusetts

March 15, 1775, 8:05 PM

Lost in thought, Finch crossed Fleet Street and was nearly run over by a carriage. He jumped out of the way just in time, but the resulting muck further dirtied his already filthy uniform.

It was a wretchedly hot day, made far worse by death, defeat, and dirt. *Truly,* Finch thought, sniffing angrily at the passing carriage, *could it get much worse?*

Of course it could.

As Finch entered the foyer to Governor Gage's mansion, he could already hear shouting. Apparently some other poor sod had beaten Finch to Governor Gage's office and was now apprising him of their military fiasco. Finch clasped his hands behind his back for the rest of the walk to Gage's office.

Finch took a deep breath, then brushed as much muck and grime as he could from his engineer's uniform. He delivered three knocks, solid and precisely spaced, against the oak door. The loud shouting on the other side of the door abruptly stopped. "Well, what are you waiting for?" came a voice. "Show the bastard in."

The door swung open. A sentinel appeared. Behind him, a weary and woebegone Major Pitcairn began threading his way out of the office. The sentinel beckoned Finch in.

Pitcairn met Finch's gaze wearily, then shook his head sadly as he brushed past Finch and limped down the hallway. Finch stepped inside.

Thomas Gage was not in good spirits. His face was red and his hair matted. He scowled at Finch but said nothing.

Finch removed his hat. His voice somber and low, he said, "The day belongs to the enemy, sir. A war is sure to follow."

"Too right it will, Major," Gage remarked sourly, "and you are, in part, to blame for it."

It seemed to Finch that Pitcairn had already taken the brunt of Gage's wrath. "Yes, sir," he replied humbly.

"Yes," Gage said. He stood up and began to pace back and forth in front of Finch, who slowly took a seat on a stool. "It is indeed upon your shoulders. You started the war with your starry-eyed idealism, entirely inappropriate when we are in conflict." He paused and sighed. "But we were not at war at the time, and you were doing your best to help. Moreover, the way Pitcairn tells it, you knew how to fight when called upon to do so." He paused, then turned and looked Finch in the eye. "I tell you this, Finch. We are in need of individuals who know how to fight, and the good Major tells me you fought like the devil. And you're just a bloody engineer!" He sat down heavily in his padded chair.

"Yes, sir. I did my best, sir."

"Your best..." Gage muttered. He leaned back in his chair, hands steepled. For several long moments he was silent.

Then he snapped out of his chair and came to his feet. "Finch? You did well on the field this day. You seem to have both a strategic and tactical mind. I would appreciate it if you could join me in my planning committee for how to fight this war."

"*SIR?!*"

chapter 2.

Preparations in Boston

Boston Harbor, Boston, Massachusetts

March 16, 1775, 10:30 AM

Finch gazed longingly at his wife, their three children, and
their wolfhound Augustus as he walked them toward the
Rainbow, bound for the English port of Bristol.

The feeling did not appear to be mutual, however. His
wife Adelaide glared back at him as she ushered the children
toward the gangplank. Finch, mindful of her disapproving
look, tried to assuage her anger. "Adelaide, the war weighs
heavily upon us all. We must make sacrifices, and it is not for
children or women to see us be killed or to watch us kill others.
It has been made clear by the dictates of society. You must
see to the children and household, whilst I serve King and
country."

Adelaide turned her delicate face away, then spoke
angrily. "Husband, you know as well as I that your argument
will not impress me. I disagree vehemently with this course of

41

action." She stopped walking, put her hands on her bony hips, and turned back to him. Her thin lips were frozen in an icy frown. "We have discussed this matter in the past at length. You promised that we would stand united and raise a family that will learn from our example."

Finch nodded. "I know, Adelaide. But I am afraid—"

"You *should* be afraid. I am most displeased to see you send me and the children abroad whilst you fight this war with neither a woman's touch nor the company of your children. Splitting this family and attending the front alone, with none of us to take care of you, and you us, is folly. Gage knows full well the value of womenfolk. He allows for wives and children to come along as followers to the camps. Yet you insist otherwise. Let me remind you that it will be very educational for the children to learn the harsh realities of life on the march."

Finch began to sputter a response, but Adelaide held a finger to his lips. "You yourself mentioned that Archibald is growing soft. You speak of the dictates of society? Constance will need to look for a husband, and would find much company amongst the officers' children and women of the camp alike. As for little Caroline, she lives for adventure. Think how much army life will indulge her in this way."

Finch smiled. He took his wife's hands in his own. "Adelaide, dearest to my heart, please understand that I would never have let this war impact us were it not in the best interests of the family. I love you all, and thus am sacrificing myself to—"

Adelaide's glare persisted. "Don't play the victim, Giles. You are not abandoning us happily, I know, and I understand why you go off to war. Yes, Gage requested that you join his council, but you also seek rank and fortune. Let that not be forgotten."

Finch paused to consider his answer. "Indeed, I do seek prestige," he said finally, "but only for the betterment of my family. As for your abandonment, I would have you be as far away from the conflict as possible. The front is a dangerous place, my love, and it is not the role of women and children to fight."

"But, when threatened, we can, and we will," Adelaide said firmly. "Are you embarrassed as to the strength and will of your own ladywife?"

Finch blushed. "Whilst I see no wrong in it, I fear it may damage my relations with the upper echelons of command."

"I see. Yet you would willingly allow the wives of others to serve?"

Finch heard himself stumbling over his words. "That is the decision of their husbands, and as master of the house, I, ehm..." Finch paused, took a breath, and began again. "Adelaide, my beloved, I humbly request that you sail with our children on the *Rainbow* and stay with my brother in Chelmsford until the conflict passes."

Finch's 15-year-old Constance hugged her father, then peered into his eyes. "Please do not order us away, Papa. We shall miss you ever so much! We love you, and your company means the world to us!"

Finch thoughtfully stroked his daughter's long, blonde hair. "I wish I need not, my darling. I love you, but know you will be better served in England, where you will be safe, and where you will find many suitors to honor you. May you find love and happiness, as well as wealth and comfort and du—"

"We'll be fine right here, Papa!" eight-year-old Caroline interrupted. "Please let us come with you! I have ever longed to see how a war is fought!"

Finch smiled at her. He patted her tightly curled hair and responded, "No doubt, Caroline, and knowing you, perhaps you may be at the front someday, whether by my desire or not, but it will not be this day. Do not despair. You will find adventures aplenty in England. Just do not worry your mother too much!"

Finch then stooped down to hug Archibald, Caroline's

twin brother, ever the silent one. He offered no response as he drew with a stick in the sand, then lifted it and threw it for Augustus to chase. The wolfhound ran off to retrieve it, barking happily.

Adelaide drew herself up haughtily. "I did not think I would see the day when you would order me about like one of Archibald's tin soldiers. But so be it. Come children. Onto the ship. Here, Gus!"

With a mixture of sorrow and relief, Finch watched his wife, children, and dog board the *Rainbow*. The ship rolled on the waves, taking on passengers in Boston Harbor, which was still closed to all mercantile vessels, as per Gage's orders.

Finch heard the clicking of shoes upon the cobblestones behind him. He turned and noted the arrival of the rest of the high council, out to see the ships off. Gage was in front, striding along, cane in hand, humming in an obvious attempt to keep his spirits up. Pitcairn, a little pale, followed, his hands clasped behind him. He was talking quietly with Grant, who, with a shoulder in a sling, looked more frail than usual. Nevertheless, he still let out a contemptuous snort every now and then. Nowhere in sight was Smith; after his near-mortal wound, he was likely being seen to by surgeons.

The faces of all Finch's fellow officers were set in grim determination. Finch knew that, like him, many of them also believed that familial separation was a necessary evil. They too were here to say goodbye to their wives and children.

One by one, they turned their gazes upon Finch, and these gazes quickly turned to glares. Because of his appointment to the high council, Finch had quickly made a few rivals, all competing for Governor Gage's good graces.

"I've served with the infantry, sir, for 30-odd years!" fumed Grant, glaring at Gage, "and now this upstart joins us as an equal? Why, he barely has seen battle at all, and, upon doing so, was simply lucky! He's good for digging holes and erecting fortresses at best! That's what I say about engineers, sir!"

Pitcairn stepped forward. "As I've been telling you, sir, this was not a matter of luck. Finch—"

"Pitcairn, Grant, shut it," Gage snapped. He turned to Grant. "Finch saw battle on many a past occasion, surveying from the front. And you're a bloody fool to dismiss a major who guided an expedition with such finesse and ingenuity. The man's a natural, and sure to be a fine staffer – as, sirs, are you both!" He looked at his officers and sniffed angrily. "Damme, gentlemen, will you cease staring upon me so? Does anyone else wish to question my decision?"

"No further objections, Governor Gage," Grant said, smirking. "Let us see how he handles himself at your mansion later today."

Governor Gage's Mansion, Boston, Massachusetts
June 16, 1775, 12:35 PM

Finch, Gage, Pitcairn, Grant, and Smith, now on the mend, sat around a conference table in one of the far-flung rooms of Governor Gage's mansion. They had spent all morning plotting, and were now continuing the conversation while eating one of the newfangled culinary delights of the Earl of Sandwich. To Finch, the "sandwiches" were neither elegant nor tasty, but he could see how placing the food of his choice between two layers of bread was a serviceable way to dine while going over battle plans.

It had been a long few months. The British were pinned down in Boston after a few abortive attempts to sally, each of which the Rebels had repulsed. Several members of the council began to clamor for a naval withdrawal to Halifax, the better to start afresh. Governor Gage, however, was decidedly opposed to this idea, as the Royal Navy did not have enough ships present to evacuate the Loyalist citizens of Boston as well. Finch and Smith threw their support behind Gage, lending the governor the confidence to turn the measure down.

Smith noted that General William Howe, a commander of some renown, was reportedly en route with a relief force. This, Smith said, gave some credibility to the idea to stand and fight. "Given time," he suggested, speaking weakly through the pain of his injury, "perhaps we might gather together a larger force and break their hold over the outskirts of town."

Finch responded by proposing an idea of his own. "Much as I like the idea of waiting until we have more men, we must assault Dorchester Heights at once. In the past few days, the enemy has built up a frightfully large force upon those hills, and their army is growing ever larger. We need to scatter them while they entrench. In doing so, we will land a tactical victory that will be sure to devastate the morale of the enemy."

The rest of the council went into an uproar. "Assault Dorchester Heights?! Without Howe?!"

Grant regarded Finch in shock, his face its usual beet red, before he began laughing in Finch's face. "Out of the question, Finch! Are you mad? General Howe's men will arrive any day now, and will bring thousands of additional soldiers to bear against our foes. If the Rebels grind down our numbers piecemeal, we could face the loss of Boston and the abandonment of our people."

Finch looked hard at Grant. "For our army to survive, we have no better alternative." He moodily took a bite out of his sandwich, chewed, stifled a gag, and swallowed. "The Rebels are emboldened by their successes. I have read disturbing news in the papers. They have gleaned enormous support from the rest of New England. Meanwhile, the other colonies look on, uneasy, and they are certainly not rendering us any aid. With the Rebels' occupation of Dorchester Heights, it will only be a matter of time before they build a string of forts atop the hills and force us from the city. We must scatter the enemy, that we might maneuver freely."

"Nonsense!" Grant retorted loudly. "Our soldiers would be slaughtered in droves as we marched up the hills. We would stand no chance against their massed fire. We must wait for Howe and more artillery, that we might have the guns to cover our advance and silence *their* cannon."

Finch raised a hand to stop the colonel's tirade. "Yes, Colonel Grant. Additional artillery pieces would be ideal. But surely you realize that any guns we could bring to bear will have minimal impact against breastworks, should we give the Rebels time to build such fortifications. At best, our cannon would suppress the enemy somewhat as we advanced."

"So, then," Grant responded angrily. "Exactly. What. Should. We. Do?"

Finch held Grant's gaze. "I heartily recommend stealth and surprise. A nighttime assault seems advisable. Tonight, even, before their fortifications are fully erected. We could advance our troops under cover of darkness and give the entrenching foe a taste of the bayonet. No shooting. We shall not only put them to flight before they can bring up any more men, but we shall impress General Howe as well. By the night's end, we will have a fine vantage point over the enemy, and over our town."

Finch paused for effect, then turned to Gage and continued. "On another note, we really must prepare for a larger-scale conflict. As our setbacks thus far have gleaned popular support for the rebellion, we must face the prospect of war across all of our holdings here in North America: from our newly-won Spanish fortresses in Florida to our humble fishing villages in northern Massachusetts. By working in concert with our navy, we could amphibiously land a series of task forces in our strongholds in the southernmost regions of the colonies. For example, Augustine Prevost and Frederick

Haldimand are stationed in Florida. What if we ask them to bring what men they can spare from the region, as well as some from the Caribbean Islands, to Saint Augustine? Once there, they can prepare to pacify any rebellious colonies in the South. Should war across the colonies break out, each of our armies could then work their way toward one another, capturing key towns along the way, as well as—"

"Peace, Finch!" Pitcairn cried good naturedly, then smiled. "I admire the bravery and guile in your attempts to hold this ground. And I certainly applaud your forward thinking. But let us consult with General Howe when he arrives, that we might ascertain what course of action he wishes to take. With our armies united, perhaps we could sail to New York and double back on foot to engage the Rebels' main columns. By occupying Manhattan and its vicinity, we could reinforce our numbers with local Loyalists and, further north, Native tribesmen. Such a conquest would also be a huge blow to the Rebellion's trade capacities with foreign nations. Meanwhile, Governor Carleton might call upon Richard Prescott and his Canadians to sally from Quebec and reinforce Fort Ticonderoga in northern New York. Perhaps they may even occupy Albany, another potential stronghold for the rebellion."

"Ah, yes, Sir Guy Carleton!" Finch exclaimed, his eyes gleaming. "Perhaps if we convince General Howe to sail to Manhattan, whilst we fight alongside Governor Gage at Dorchester tonight, and persuade Governor Carleton to send troops down from Canada, we might be able to contain this vile insurgency before it spreads."

"Perhaps we should simply evacuate to the deep south after all," Gage said, growing impatient. "Much as I hate to leave my constituents, we can take a number of refugees with us once the transports bearing Howe's men arrive. It is a distance from the opposition, and since it is unlikely the Rebels will be able to invade Canada, perhaps we could join forces with Prevost and Haldimand in the southern colonies. With them, we can force our way back northward in great numbers, garnering further manpower from the local Loyalists."

"Unfortunately, a rather poor idea, General," said Smith, rising from his place at the table and briefly cringing in pain from his wounds. "I am in favor of Finch's plan, with an alteration. First, however, permit me to rebut your proposition. The South may have many Loyalists and the grounds to train them, but when they hear that we ran from battle up north, they would be loath to fight alongside us, for fear of us faltering yet again. We would, furthermore, be unable to contain the Rebellion's twisted ideologies; they will run amok throughout the northern territories, gather more support, and also give the enemy additional time to train their men. Finch is right. We must strike quickly before the enemy manages to muster and organize troops."

Gage pondered the idea, his hand on his chin. After a time, he nodded. "Very well. You mentioned that you supported Finch's idea, but with an alteration. What alteration would you make, sir?"

Smith coughed into his fist and sat down again. "Finch suggested we stay in Boston and assault Dorchester Heights in the dark of night. I agree with this suggestion. We both also agree with Pitcairn's idea that Prescott should sally from Canada to reinforce Fort Ticonderoga. However, my adaptations are twofold: first, that although Prescott should occupy Fort Ticonderoga, he should not push his force any further into New York from there. If we can keep the focus of the conflict on the New England territories alone, I feel that it would be much to our advantage. We do not wish to risk the outrage of the mid-Atlantic colonials."

Smith paused, easing back in his chair, and massaged the dressing on his wound. "Though we should attack Dorchester

Heights tonight, not waiting for General Howe, I suggest that, once he arrives, we join forces with him in Boston, rather than sail to Manhattan. We may need reinforcements during the battle, or additional manpower in the defense of Boston in the case of a counterattack. What's more, if the Rebels scatter, we shall need a fresh reserve force to unleash upon the retreating enemy."

Grant wiped his brow. It looked to Finch as though he was going to speak rudely, but instead he smiled grimly. "You have done some thinking, Smith," he admitted.

"We all did, Colonel Grant."

Grant nodded.

"*SIR!*" came a cry from outside the door.

"Enter!" Gage shouted over his shoulder.

A messenger, his face stubbled, clothes drenched from a stormy morning at sea, stepped forth with a dispatch. "Letter from Lord Dunmore."

"The governor of Virginia?" Gage said. "Give it here." He grabbed the paper and pored over it as Finch, Grant, Smith, and Pitcairn stood by, waiting anxiously.

"I wonder what Dunmore would want with—" Grant began.

"Gentlemen," Gage interrupted, "we have a conundrum."

All eyes were focused on Gage now. He was frowning mightily. He said, "John Murray, Lord Dunmore, has publicly promised the immediate emancipation of any slave owned by a Rebel landowner if that slave agrees to fight for the Crown. He is alienating slave owners on both sides of the conflict, all in order to build a personal army to defend his governorship." Gage looked from commander to commander. "He asks for our help – an escort for him and his troops out of Virginia and into the north, where they can rearm, train, and rest."

There was a brief, shocked silence.

"Good God!" Grant said, his face screwed into a grimace.

"The man must be stopped! Brought to justice at once before the bloody Negroes run wild!"

"Calmly, Grant, calmly," Finch said evenly through gritted teeth. "I admire Lord Dunmore his initiative. He has excited a populace to arms against an injustice that has long plagued society – an injustice that has already been outlawed in England."

Smith grunted. "Enacting such a policy in Virginia will surely make things difficult for him."

"Aye," Finch admitted. "Virginia is a bellicose colony that will fight to the last to protect landowners' right to own slaves. What's more, he will not win over all the slaves, for some will maintain their allegiance to their Rebel masters. Others will not be freed because their masters are Loyalists. Moreover, by freeing slaves, Lord Dunmore will rouse many otherwise neutral or even Loyal white southerners to arms against him."

"You would help him, Finch?" Gage inquired, his eyebrow cocked.

Finch hesitated, weighing his options. "Yes, sir," he said finally. "I recommend sending troops to evacuate him and his men, regardless of color."

Smith looked at Finch in shock.

"Consider this," Finch continued. "It may also be an opportunity to gain the trust and allegiance of the Negro populace and expose the hypocrisy of the Rebel cause to their potential allies, such as the French, the Spanish, or anyone else who means us harm. They claim to fight for freedom, yet they keep untold numbers of human beings in bondage. Providing safe passage and harbor for John Murray and his troops may enable us to garner international approval. It may also begin the next phase in our empire's path toward slavery's abolition since the mother country's abolition of the practice in 1772." Finch paused and took a long breath. "Let us escort Lord Dunmore and his men to Boston, where we can make good use of the additional troops. And let us not compel the beleaguered governor to breach his promise."

Gage smiled condescendingly. "Ever the idealist, eh, Finch?"

Finch blushed. "I merely hope to live to see the day when we measure a man solely by his personality and merits."

Gage coughed, perhaps hiding a smile. "Colonel Smith, your opinion?"

Rubbing his arm, Smith said, "Best to send a detachment to escort and then detain Lord Dunmore, sir. Recall him, and consolidate our forces whilst he faces trial. We can't have his blacks running amok in Virginia, meting a vengeance against their masters. Certainly isn't fair that they were enslaved – a horrible fate for anyone – but we also cannot trust them to wander free in the middle of a war. John Murray don't have the discipline to keep them under control. The only way to unite them would be to keep them constantly engaged with the Rebels."

Pitcairn cleared his throat and stood. "Smith mostly has the right of it. However, Lord Dunmore's word to his people is his bond. We should be supportive and helpful to Governor Murray, and uphold the freedom of those he has manumitted, so long as he frees no more men without express permission from Horse Guards."

Grant stared at Gage, but pointed at Finch. "While Finch may have the right of it in the eyes of our Lord and Savior," he said, "we cannot afford to risk the outrage of the southerners, sir. Lord Dunmore's stance will bring many a hopeful Negro to our doorstep. Should we welcome them, I will have no objection, but such activity will no doubt anger the Virginian plantation owners. And it could turn all the colonies against us."

Gage steepled his fingers and frowned. Speaking slowly, he said, "I do not believe that what Lord Dunmore did was morally wrong. Though it was perhaps legally wrong, such transgressions are often part of the nature of war. However, due to the hamstrung nature of our forces, we will be unable to help him in the middle colonies. When General Howe arrives, we shall send for Lord Dunmore, using the ships that conveyed Howe's men here. These will transport Dunmore and his men, both white and black, to New England. Here, his fate shall be decided. Let us hope that he holds against the enemy until our ships arrive. Perhaps in the meantime he might learn some humility and common sense. We can only pray that he will not rouse too many Virginians to outrage."

Gage stood and looked slowly around the room. "Gentlemen, the game is afoot. We attack tonight. The enemy will be entrenching their position, and I am convinced that the Rebels, not being possessed of the bayonet, will be at a distinct disadvantage in a melee. If we approach with stealth, we shall catch them off guard, overrun their position, and greet General Howe and his admiral brother from our vantage point with a gun salute soon afterward." He put his hands on the table. "You have your orders, gentlemen. Let us begin."

Governor Gage's Mansion, Boston, Massachusetts
June 16, 1775, 7:35 PM

As the day wore on, Finch assisted Gage in managing other affairs regarding the colony of Massachusetts. On three occasions, they were interrupted by anxious Loyalist town leaders, who had noticed the Rebels beginning to reinforce their position on the hills south of Boston. Finch explained curtly to each one that the Rebels' efforts had been well noticed and would be dealt with in the proper time. He added that every effort was being made toward ensuring the Loyalists' safety here in Boston.

As the sun began to set, a messenger arrived with the latest report from Halifax. Gage read it eagerly, an excited expression upon his face.

"Ah, Finch!" he exulted, his eyes aglow. "It seems our support has nearly arrived! Read this!" He handed Finch the letter.

Finch adjusted his spectacles and gazed upon the spidery writing of Francis Legge, governor of New Scotland.

April 27th, 1775

Dear Thomas Gage, Commandant of British forces in Boston,

I, Francis Legge, beg to report that the naval elements led by Admiral Richard Howe and Captain Samuel Drake, numbering among the following vessels attached to this dispatch, have sent forth from Halifax and are en route to Boston.

This fleet conveys an army under General William Howe, Richard's brother. He has arrayed a force of four thousand men among the line infantry, with five hundred grenadiers, five hundred light infantrymen, a battalion of two hundred and forty marines, four hundred and eighty horse, four guns, and supply in support. They are meant to reinforce your garrison.

Be advised: said fleet shall make port with black sails, for, most unfortunately, the ships did hit poor weather, and many a good man did not arrive in New Scotland, having been buried at sea.

With best wishes,
LEGGE
Governor, Royal Province of New Scotland

Finch returned the letter to Gage, who kissed it in relief. "Thank goodness for the men, whatever shape they are in. I am sure they will prove useful."

chapter 3.
Assaulting Dorchester Heights

June 16, 1775, 8:33 PM

Dread filled Finch as he and his fellow officers prepared for battle, which Gage had ordered to begin at precisely 11 o'clock that night. An hour before, Finch had hurriedly penned a heartfelt letter to Adelaide, whom he hoped was now in Chelmsford with his elder brother Jacob:

> *June 16, 1775*
>
> *My dear Adelaide, love of my life,*
>
> *I offer you my utmost admiration and adoration, this day and always. I trust you have made your way safely to Chelmsford and are now enjoying the hospitality of my brother. Is he well? How is the rest of the family? I do hope Caroline and Gus have not gotten into more trouble than is healthy, and that Constance is showered with admiration by many a potential suitor. Has Archibald shown more interest in his studies? What are your*

hopes and dreams of late, and how may I help you achieve them at this distance?

Please know that in the days ahead, we will be undergoing offensive operations against the Rebellion. There is some chance of my undoing. Know that if I do fall, that I adored you all well, and that I put my life on the line less for our glorious King and Country and more to preserve our family name and ensure that the rest of you have a goodly life.

With a love that outshines the fiery steeds of Helios himself, there is not one day that goes by in which I do not yearn for you.

Your husband,
  Giles Finch

PS. In my reminiscences, I always hear the tune that brought us together in dance. However, I must admit I have forgotten the song's title. Could you tell me its name?

After sending the letter, Finch was now able to focus with a healthy conscience on the battle ahead. The soldiers were were willing, ready for action, and humbled by their earlier encounters at Lexington and Concord. They would do their job bravely and with less overconfidence this time. Yet Finch knew that his men faced a challenging task. Overwhelming a high-ground position was always dangerous, especially by night, when men could easily become lost. This was made still more possible by a mist that had arisen after sunset. This would necessitate the movement of Crown troops in close order until they were near the top of the hill. That would help for matters of navigation and morale, but woe betide them should the surprised enemy manage an effective volley.

A surprise attack was essential to gaining Dorchester Heights. Finch knew that the British lights and grenadiers were capable of speed and nimble maneuvering tactics, and he assumed that the hat companies would hold their own. But he worried deeply about the abilities of the Loyalist militia, who had expressed a great desire to join in the surprise attack.

Yet how could he and the other officers have said anything but yes to their offer? Finch feared that the little-trained auxiliaries would be too slow or faint of heart to be of any real service, and that they might even hamper the closed ranks of the British troops. But he also knew that to disallow the honest Tory from a role in the public defense would further harm His Majesty's relations with the colonies. After discussing the matter, all the commanders had embraced the patriotism of the King's loyal colonial subjects and welcomed them into their ranks.

In a few hours, they would know how wise or foolish a decision that would be.

Roxbury Hill, Boston, Massachusetts

June 17, 1775, 11:20 AM

Finch looked at the threadbare line of Loyalist militiamen attributed to his command. Each of the roughly 300 men was equipped with some manner of a melee weapon and a fowling piece, as well as 18 rounds in his cartridge box.

Finch turned to Pitcairn, who was commanding the light infantry, and nodded grimly. He started to speak, but Pitcairn shook his head.

"Not a word, Giles. We'll get through this together."

Finch offered a sickly smile in return, then took the head of his hastily convened regiment of Massachusetts and New Hampshire Loyalists. Some looked angry and determined; others quivered in terror. Finch hoped that none would turn and run at the first volley.

What remained of the Lexington and Concord Expedition waited nearby, along with the redcoats of the Boston garrison, ready to receive marching orders. Professional light infantry were assembled on the immediate left and right of Finch's force. With the militia, these men made up the entirety of a left flank. Hat companies formed the center, and grenadiers created the right flank. It was a somewhat traditional battle formation with a slight alteration that Gage had suggested, placing the militia between companies of professional lights, in order to better bolster the Loyalists' morale.

Suddenly, a whispered command went up and down the ranks. The order had been given to commence the march up the hill.

On the hilltop, Finch could see the Rebel watch fires, illuminating the mist. He shivered in the clammy night air, then drew his watchcoat close around himself and turned to one of his captains, a New Hampshire man named Timothy Lawrence.

"Time to go, Captain," Finch said softly. "We have a meeting with fate. Keep closed ranks. We don't want to lose anyone in this mist."

"Yes sir," was the whispered reply.

And so it began.

The forces of the Crown and their Loyalist allies sallied into the brush covering Roxbury Hill. Stepping quickly, they climbed upward.

As the watch fires grew ever nearer, Finch ordered his men to disperse amongst the trees and stealthily make their way to the hilltop.

Soon Finch could make out the outlines of Rebel troops huddled around the fires. Others were digging deep into the ground with shovels, creating what seemed to be the beginning of a series of entrenchments. The Rebel soldiers looked as miserable as the men of the Crown did, and for a fleeting second, Finch allowed himself a touch of sympathy for his foes.

Then, as the British troops came over the crest of the hill, attempting to conceal themselves amongst the trees, a cry went up in the Rebel camp.

"Sound the alarm! We're under attack!"

Finch immediately noticed the Rebel soldier who had spoken. He had looked up from his digging and caught sight of the red coats of the line infantry.

Heeding the young man's terrified shout, the minutemen began to form ranks, snare drums rattling and fifes warbling. Those who were off duty ran for their muskets.

Thunder rumbled menacingly. Seconds later, a rain began to fall.

"Fire at will!" came the cries of sergeants from both sides.

Soldiers made ready to discharge their firelocks, but because the damp weather had moistened their flints and steel, few pieces went off on either side. Instead, there was much cursing from the professional soldiers, panicked shouting from the volunteers, and bracing cries from the commanding officers.

At first, only a few men fell on either side. Then, the British center was rocked by a robust series of shots from the Rebel militia. Ensnarled by the trees, lost in the darkness, and now under heavy fire, the hatmen wavered.

Gage took the opportunity to make a hero of himself. "Come, lads!" he yelled suddenly from a position to Finch's right. He flourished his blade. "Our ammunition is wet and our muskets ineffectual. We're going to charge them!" Gage looked about his force and Finch could have sworn the governor gave him a wink as his gaze swept past. "Gentlemen! Charge bayonets!"

"*HUZZAH!*" came the roar of a thousand redcoats as

they lowered their blades, backed by their auxiliaries from the colonies.

"Come lads!" Finch shouted. "You heard the governor! Attack!"

After milling about for a few seconds, the Loyalist militiamen rallied themselves to strike as one with their crude collection of cudgels, hatchets, and daggers.

The Rebels, hearing the cries of the enemy and seeing the glint of British bayonets in the moonlight, quickly began to panic. Over the moans of agony and the clashes of steel on steel, Finch heard shouts of "Fall back!"

Suddenly, a Rebel soldier hurried toward Finch, swinging his musket like a club. Finch grimly plunged his blade into the man's stomach, then kicked him off his saber and stepped aside to let his victim fall.

Catching his breath, Finch allowed himself a look around the battlefield. The Rebels appeared to be in trouble already, having been taken unawares by the well-organized attack. Now they were forced into a melee where they no longer had the advantage of higher ground. Some were already quitting the field, leaving behind their muskets and powder. Finch even saw a team of horses being unhitched from an artillery piece, so the horses could be ridden away by separate riders. Where they had garnered such guns, Finch could not even guess.

Finch quickly checked the pan of his pistol to see if it was loaded, then turned to his militia. "Onward, lads! This fight is not yet won. Let us take a few of the enemy's colors! You all will be accessories to our collective triumph! Stick to the mists and smoke, lads! Let the grenadiers cover our advance! We will snake past their charge and make a mad dash for the center of the enemy camp. Deprived of their colors, they'll have neither a rally point nor honor!"

The men stared at Finch blankly. He groaned inwardly. *Show, don't tell.*

He shouted, "Converged militia! Front march! Keep the grenadiers between us and the enemy!"

Finch and the New Hampshire and Massachusetts Loyalists hurried forward. The thin red line of grenadiers and hatmen were heavily engaged in a melee at the time, so no other officer protested this maneuver. Their approach was masked by the sounds of combat, the smoke of the watch fires, and the rain and mist. Finch and his men snaked around the general engagement and crept toward the camp. Progress was slow, but Finch was convinced that their actions would further undermine the enemy's already devastated morale.

As the camp swam into view past the mist and smoke, Finch was able to make out a ramshackle officers' hut, a score of tents, and a few firepits. Nowhere could he see an enemy regiment, much less the colors of one. It seemed as though the base was all but abandoned.

Ptch! Krak! Ptch!

The smell of gunpowder assaulted Finch's nostrils as he dove for cover. Smoke from a pair of misfires and a missed shot billowed out of the officers' cabin, while more enemy soldiers suddenly made their appearance from behind the cover of their tents.

"No time to shoot back, lads!" Finch bellowed. "Charge those men! I want that camp cleared!"

Even as he ordered this advance, however, Finch could not help but fire a shot of his own at the window of the officers' cabin. As he expected, the moist powder did not take to the flame when the flint and steel snapped together.

Finch put away his pistol and drew his blade. Then, motioning to Captain Lawrence and a pair of his soldiers to follow him, Finch ran toward the cabin.

When they arrived at its door, the four attempted to force it open, but it would not budge. Finch saw that the door was thick, reinforced, and probably blocked.

Finch thought of the big field gun that he had seen abandoned just a few minutes before. He wondered briefly if it would be possible to pivot the gun and blast open the door.

Suddenly, over the mayhem of battle, a voice spoke loudly from inside the cabin.

"Parley!"

"Why, what do you want of us?" Finch replied, gesturing his command to stand down.

The voice from indoors said firmly, "I, Captain Godfrey, of the Rhode Island Militia, would like to surrender myself to the hospitality of the Crown forces. You have my men on the run, and I am all but defenseless."

Finch smiled, pleased to have captured a ranking officer in battle. "Very well, Captain, we are coming in. Please instruct your men to place their weapons on the ground and be prepared to surrender your hanger blade."

Captain Lawrence spoke up suddenly. "Let me take him in, sir. My family has never been very successful in the art of war. I must redeem them!"

Finch pondered the matter for a few moments, then turned to Lawrence. "Very well, Lawrence. Let's be quick and clean about this, yes?"

"Yes, sir."

Finch and Lawrence tried once more to open the door, only to find that their entrance remained blocked. After five exhausting minutes working in tandem with the two additional militiamen, the engineer and his cohort finally broke through the heavy oak door. As the door fell with a crash, it revealed a room relieved of most its accoutrements, with only a desk and bed remaining. Through an open window, Finch saw the retreating backs of a few Rebel soldiers.

"Blast!" Lawrence hissed. He pounded the oaken desk with his fist.

Finch sighed. "No matter. Let us return to our men."

They went back outside, where a steady stream of Rebel soldiers was stampeding past them. Looking around, Finch saw that the Rebel entrenchment detail and their reinforcements had been beaten. The enemy was on the run. *This is my time to shine in the glory of the sun,* Finch thought. He hurried to the center of the Rebel encampment, where he found his small force of Loyalists ransacking the tents.

"What are you doing, lads?" Finch shouted. "The enemy is on the retreat! We must seize captives!"

"But, sir," one of the militiamen replied "We put the enemies present to flight. Isn't that enough? Didn't you tell us to seize the battle standards?"

Finch sighed. The man had a point. He looked around wildly for an enemy to charge or stab. There was none. The entire Rebel force had fled..

Finch spotted Gage and hurried over to him. "What is the plan now, sir?"

Gage grunted, surveying the battlefield. "Well, Finch, the Rebels have been defeated. They are surely terrorized and exhausted, so we shall continue the push to liberate the enemy's position in the neighboring heights. Press the advantage, you see. Grant and I will brush the enemy away from the high ground entirely. From there, we hope their leaders will resign their commissions in disgrace and terror." He looked at Finch. "As for you, Major, pick ten men and survey the fallen for signs of life. Evacuate those you can to safety. The Rebels included. Let it never be said the Crown did not take care of Her prisoners. After that, we shall continue the entrenchment of this hill, under your command."

Finch nodded. "Yes, sir." He set out to gather a collection of grenadiers to do the unpleasant work.

By the time the sky began to lighten, Finch and his men had found 68 British and Loyalist troops dead or wounded.

But the Rebels had lost over 200 – and who knew how many had been wounded but had managed to escape?

When the sun peeked over the horizon, an exhausted Finch sat, hat in hand, upon the hastily erected fortifications overlooking the Massachusetts countryside.

Finch's bosom swelled with a grim sort of pride to think that he was, in part, responsible for the success of the day. He drew out his spyglass, held it to his eye, and watched with satisfaction as Rebel forces on nearby Watertown Hill began to withdraw. Presumably, their commander, Artemas Ward, had recognized that their position was now untenable.

Best of all, the Crown army had managed to triumph without Howe.

For all their success, Finch nonetheless grieved as he watched men on both sides being cast into mass graves. Though the Rebels of Massachusetts had the worst of it, there must have been at least 30 men fighting under the standard of a single small New Hampshire contingent who were laid to rest in those makeshift burial grounds. Scores more from all across New England were entombed beneath the earth with them.

A quick look at the state of his own side, however, reminded Finch that he need not feel solely responsible for the carnage of the morning. The hatmen of the Fifty-Fifth Foot alone had suffered 14 dead and wounded, struck by one of the only successful volleys fired by either side.

For now, Finch hid his grief and exhaustion. He kept up an appearance of professionalism as he barked orders at his men, who carried the wounded to safety in the officers' hut, which they had turned into a makeshift field hospital.

Many of the soldiers' musketball wounds were especially grievous. Bones were crushed, flesh was burnt and torn, and Finch knew that poisoning from the lead was all but inevitable. Those men lucky enough to survive would live out their lives with disfiguring and painful injuries. As Finch watched, several wounded men were deemed still fit for combat by the end of the day, pending a rest. But by the looks upon their faces at this announcement, Finch guessed that many would have preferred to die immediately.

As the sun rose crimson in the early morning sky, Finch noted that the last of the casualties had been cleared from the field of battle. His work was not done, however. He and a few men from each battalion now faced the task of erecting breastworks to repulse any future Rebel assaults.

Governor Gage's Mansion, Boston, Massachusetts
June 17, 1775, 12:45 PM

To celebrate their victory over the Rebels at Dorchester, as well as the imminent arrival of General Howe and Admiral Howe, Governor Gage hosted a lunch for the council. It was to be a joyous affair, and Gage had insisted that Finch briefly leave the fortification of the hills to Captain Simmons and join in the good cheer.

All manner of delicious dishes, from artichokes and apples to turkey, partridges, and sirloin roast, were prepared for the occasion. As Finch and his colleagues ate, they talked of their families and regaled each other with tales of their military careers.

"What about you, Finch?" Smith inquired. "Got any exciting tales to lend to our discussion?"

Finch energetically began to share a tale of his adventures alongside General Howe at the battle of Quebec. Then the door to the room suddenly flew open, after which there was a moment of stillness and silence.

A tall, slim gentleman with a crop of brown hair and

an aristocratic face strode into Gage's conference room with great dignity. William Howe was dressed in a well-kept officer's uniform belonging to the Royal Welch Fusiliers – a red coat with blue collars and cuffs, bedecked with gold lace.

Finch rose to his feet quickly, ready to offer his deepest respects.

A rotund captain sidled up behind the general and took his coat. "Gentlemen," he began meekly, "I present to you General William Howe."

"Why, General Howe!" cried Governor Gage, extending his arms in greeting, perhaps a bit too enthusiastically. "What an honor to see you safely arrived. Welcome to Boston, and may I say, it is a pleasure to see you again!"

General Howe simply nodded. If he recognized Finch, he did not betray this fact. "Gentlemen," he said, his voice barely above a whisper. "Please forgive the absence of my brother, as well as Generals Burgoyne and Clinton. They are all down with the flu. It was a very difficult journey. I hear you are to be congratulated this day. You have dispersed a force that has, in the past, outmatched and outnumbered your own. However, now my men are here to aid you in this time of need. Follow my example, and together we shall restore order to this land in as peaceable a manner as we can. Then we can all go home to our wives and children."

There was a pause, followed by some polite applause, after which Finch wondered why he had clapped at all. Howe's words had been less than inspiring. Yet Finch knew that Howe was a gifted officer when roused to arms. *Howe will eventually show his allies his worth*, Finch thought. *There can be no doubt about that.*

Governor Gage's Mansion, Boston, Massachusetts

June 17, 1775, 3:05 PM

After a long and hearty meal, Gage dismissed his other officers, but he called upon Finch to stay behind, that the two might test each other's wits in a game of chess. Finch knew that he had no option but to comply, though he also knew that he was needed atop Roxbury Hill.

As the game drew to a close, Gage grew frustrated. The chessmen at his command had dwindled considerably, including the loss of his queen. His initial response was, therefore, one of relief when there was a knock at the door.

"Enter," the governor replied with gusto, standing with a flourish of his hand to the guard at the door.

The door creaked open to reveal Howe in all his regal glory. He stepped inside and said, "Gentlemen. I am glad to find you well. Though I fear I must single out General Gage for conversation at this time. Major, you may go."

Finch stood to leave, but Gage, catching the expression on Howe's face, shook his head. He seemed to know what this was about, though he did not reveal it at once. "Respectfully, General, if you wish to discuss the matter at hand, know that Finch is a trusted confidant. We can confer on the matter in front of him."

Howe squared his shoulders. "Very well. I shall speak plainly. I have looked over the reports and dispatches you have sent to Horse Guards. It is a shame that you failed to negotiate acceptably with the populace you have oppressed so." Howe crossed the room and seated himself in Gage's vacant desk chair. Gage bowed his head in recognition of Howe's authority.

Howe continued as though he were unaware of Gage's reaction. "I assure you, however, that I will do my utmost to restore goodwill between the colonies and the Crown. Because

Daniel H Lessin

of your initial approaches to the problem, we may see some complications and combat, but we shall minimize casualties for all in the process." Howe cleared his throat and now showed a bit of uneasiness. "My brother's vessels are damaged after their long, hard journey, but as soon as they are properly patched up, we shall see you on your way."

"Sir," Gage said, "do you mean to say—"

Howe nodded. "I do. Your years of inability to put down the rebellion or negotiate a solution have come to a head, and the King has called for your replacement and dismissal."

"But surely my knowledge of the colonies could be of use?" Gage asked, half pleading, half angry.

"Lord George Germain has made his views quite clear, sir. You may leave."

Gage was barely able to contain his rage. "I…understand, General. Forgive me, I must repair to my quarters to pack, if you will not be needing me further. Good evening, sir." The humiliated governor stood and hurried out of the room, shaking his head.

Finch could not help but smile for the first time in weeks. This was his opportunity, as a staffer under Gage, to return to Chelmsford. He would no longer be stuck in an endless conflict and could once again attend to his family.

Keeping his eyes averted, Finch moved to follow his employer out the door, bowing as he passed General Howe.

Howe smiled. "While I envy your devotion to your employer, Major Finch, you have not been dismissed. Nor may anyone else leave my command without resigning their commission."

Damme. He stopped and turned to face Howe.

"At your service, sir," Finch replied meekly. "It has been some time. How can I be of assistance to you?"

Howe examined Finch with interest for the first time. "It

is good to see you again, Major. I see the years have treated you well. A mercy, to be sure." He smiled.

Finch repressed a cringe. He had seen that smile before.

"It appears you have not been living off your laurels since the Plains of Abraham," Howe continued. "Working as hard as ever, I see. You are keeping close to your government. This is a wondrous good thing."

"Thank you, General Howe. Have you been well, sir?"

"Thinking freely," the general said, smiling again. "A notion of mixed merits. It may not garner one personal glory, but it may well save the day. I've been governing the Isle of Wight, whilst my representation of Nottingham in Parliament goes as planned. Under the circumstances, of course, you realize."

There was a knock at the door.

"Ehm, yes. Certainly, sir. Challenging times we live in."

"Enter," Howe said loudly.

A servant – evidently one of Howe's – entered with tea on a tray. Finch reached for a cup to steady himself.

Howe took a cup of his own. "Indeed." He leaned forward and looked into Finch's eyes. "I don't want this position. I don't believe in this fight, and I do not believe we can win in a prolonged conflict. Nonetheless, King George commands me, and here I am. It is my duty to serve."

Finch nodded.

"You're the ranking engineer in town, are you not?"

Finch nodded. "Yes, sir. At your service."

"So it was you who planned Boston's defenses, too, then?"

"I did my best, sir."

"Your best," Howe mused, taking his time to look Finch over. After a few moments' pause, he spoke again, looking Finch straight in the eye. "Sir, your entrenchments are shallow and the blockhouses shoddily constructed. Yet I need your help. What say you to that?"

"Sir," Finch replied, turning red in the face, "we have completed only the most basic defenses of Boston. My corps was ordered to abandon our labors and rest in preparation for the fortification of Dorchester Heights, which we have just assaulted and brought to heel."

Howe bit his lip as he regarded Finch, pondering this new information. "An assault. I see. And who suggested this sally, the better to defend so quaint and beauteous a town?"

Finch squared his jaw. "General, it is time to bring you up to speed with the situation of late."

Roxbury Hill, Boston, Massachusetts
June 17, 1775, 5:03 PM

It was a harrowing hike up Roxbury Hill – for Finch, the second climb in the past day, with the ghosts of the last one still haunting him. Though he did not wish to fight this war, and deeply wished to instead be with his family, he understood the importance of providing them with honor and fortune. The best way to accomplish this, he knew, would be to quell the rebellion.

With Howe walking by his side, he felt sure that victory would come soon – decisively. But he felt remorseful leaving Governor Gage, who also could benefit from such honor, out of the fight. Gage had done as well as could be expected, both as a military governor and as a diplomat. It was not his fault that Hancock and his Sons of Liberty were unreasonable.

Still reeling from the events of the past few days, Finch addressed Howe, gesturing toward what had been the battlefield. "This is where we scattered the Rebels to the wind. General Gage did a spectacular job of holding the line with his men, whilst the rest of us swept up along the Rebel flanks and hammered them." He took a long breath. "When it became clear that firelocks were useless in such conditions, Gage, not to be outdone by the professional soldiery, led his men in a charge. *With Loyalist militia, sir.* I've led provincials in a charge before, as you recall, at the Plains of Abraham, and such men are known to waver, so one would expect untrained auxiliaries to run at the first shot. Yet Gage, consummate leader that he is, carried the day. He fought hard. He did well to bring the Loyalists to the cause in the first place, and then kept them alongside the rest of the men in the fight."

Howe nodded but said nothing.

Finch continued, "Sir, Governor Gage is a man of valor. He should not be sent home. I strongly advise that you permit the governor to continue to help quell the Rebellion on behalf of the nation we so love."

Howe surveyed the scene, his hands on his hips. "Well," he said finally. "at least Gage's men are loyal. I shall write a letter to Horse Guards and request that he continue his tour of duty here in America. Perhaps he shall retain governorship over Massachusetts as well. I will tell him upon our return." He smiled. "I have received word that the Rebels have retreated not only to the south and west, but northward as well. We shall have some work to do."

Howe drew his coat about him as he walked through the battlefield. He looked down at the newly dug entrenchments ordered by Finch, including a dugout for the newly captured artillery piece and the foundations for two blockhouses. To Finch's surprise, he inspected the defenses thoughtfully and silently for several minutes.

At length, General Howe spoke. "Finch? These will be some fine fortifications. Carry on."

"Yes, sir," Finch said.

"The enemy has withdrawn, and it is time we commence a cautious pursuit. We must ensure the locals, who largely mean us no harm, that we are here to help them against a terrifying partisan force that stalks their land. You and General Gage will assist me. Is that clear?"

"Yes, sir," Finch said again.

chapter 4.
The Massachusetts Campaign

June 30, 1775, 8:33 AM

At long last, Howe's top officers had joined Gage's at the governor's mansion to discuss the conflict ahead.

Seated at the table next to Finch was the brave but bombastic General Henry Clinton. Across from them, between Pitcairn and Howe, sat the charismatic playboy actor and dragoon officer, John Burgoyne. Clinton and Burgoyne were a colorful pair who, Finch quickly realized, were often at odds. To Finch, they seemed just as willing to duel each other as they were to fight the Rebels.

Several of the officers were excited to begin the campaign and prove themselves to the Crown. Others, including Finch, sorrowfully sipped their tea and wished they were elsewhere.

Howe stood at the front of the room, gesturing at a map posted behind him. His aide-de-camp, the rotund captain who had announced Howe's arrival, scribbled notes with a quill upon parchment. Finch realized suddenly that he had yet to ask the captain's name.

"Governor Gage," Howe said, "your impressive rout of the revolutionaries has caused them to divide their forces into three columns, each roughly the size of your own fighting force. With the reinforcement of your fellows by my command, we now have a formidable army. We can easily overcome any single column we choose. And this assumes that the enemy is comprised of professionally trained troops. Yet, they are not. They are mostly farmers, easily conquered in battle, and we have them on the run. Their morale must be terribly low. I doubt they shall be able to hold out beyond another battle or two before their courage fails them. Then we shall restore their sense of civic duty."

Howe leaned forward and reached toward a platter of scones in the table's center. He selected one and took a bite before continuing. "With the assistance of Generals Burgoyne, Clinton, and Gage, I shall take the helm of this army. We shall offer solace and protection to those in need, occupying major towns with small relief garrisons, and chasing down the main enemy column." Howe paused and took a second bite. "This column belongs to their commander- in- chief, a former Virginia provincial by the name of George Washington."

Finch let out a snort. "They put *him* in charge, sir? The Rebels must be more desperate than we previously thought." Washington had a reputation for being reckless and overly confident. Finch remembered well the tense days from the war against the French when he and Washington, along with Washington's token force of provincials, had patrolled the frontier territories between French and British America.

Howe coughed and smiled. "If Mister Finch would permit me to continue."

Finch blushed. "Apologies, sir."

Howe resumed. "Washington, having taken command

from Artemas Ward's provisional authority, has fallen back northward. We shall pursue him in that direction, but we will not chase the fox into the mid-Atlantic. We shall try to keep this fiasco a strictly New England affair. Colonel Fin—"

"Ah, that's Major Finch, sir," Finch said.

Howe raised an eyebrow. "You're a colonel now, sir. Gage told me it was your idea to liberate Dorchester Heights. You saved us from having to evacuate Boston, and I daresay you could be of great use to me as an advisor. You will come with me." He turned to the other end of the table. "Colonel Smith?"

The colonel looked blearily at Howe, then saluted clumsily.

"You are clearly still suffering from your wounds. Rest yourself in Boston, sir. I shall place you in garrison command of the Forty-Third Foot, with the responsibility of training the local Bostonians into a force of provincial soldiers. Loyalist militia simply will not do any longer, Sir."

Smith saluted again. "Yes, sir. Thank you, sir. The Loyalists will be ready."

"Major Pitcairn," Howe continued. "I hear tell that you are much like me – a man of peace and goodwill toward the colonies."

Pitcairn blinked, then nodded. "Yes, sir, I am, but I am also a soldier, sir."

"Indeed," Howe said. "Now, I want you to lead a small force to Newport, over here, in the colony of Rhode Island." Howe tapped the map with his baton. "Coerce the colonials there to cease their wild behavior. They are making a misguided effort to challenge our maritime dominance. They will only embarrass themselves when they are bested by my brother Richard. His ships of the line will accompany you on this mission." Howe flashed a sudden smile at Pitcairn. "You will like Dick. He, too, means the colonies no excessive harm and wishes for harmony and reconciliation between the two factions."

Howe coughed and moved his baton down the map. "In the meantime, frigates and transports under Captain Drake will rescue the forces of Lord Dunmore from Virginia, which are now on the outskirts of Norfolk, and will transport them north to Newport, rather than to Boston." Howe paused and sighed.

"I am not fond of this decision, for the Governor had no right to liberate the property of his constituents, but I shall abide by Governor Gage's demands." He looked intently at Gage, then returned his gaze to Pitcairn. "Until Lord Dunmore's most...colorful force arrives, however, I fear your expedition's strength will be restricted to marines from our nearby vessels of war, as well as any refugees from the surrounding settlements. However, I understand that Lord Dunmore's Virginian command has swelled to a great size. I trust that you can discipline, billet, and train them, as well as send them into battle."

"Of course, sir," Pitcairn said, his voice laden with uncertainty.

Colonel Grant spoke up urgently. "What about me, General Howe?"

There was an awkward silence as Howe turned and glared at Colonel Grant.

"Colonel, I have heard about the lack of leadership you showed during the scuffle that ensued during the most recent powder alarm. Your actions were cause for great distress in their own right."

Grant stuttered as he searched for his words. "Why, I...I...I disarmed the settlement and escorted to Boston a band of refugees. Of what distress do you speak?"

After a moment's silence, Howe responded. He spoke calmly – but Finch, having known Howe for a time, could see the fury in his eyes. "I speak, Sir, of your blatant disregard for colonial property and life. Your actions – shooting a young civilian in cold blood and destroying private property the better to dispose of an enemy supply depot, show a taste for gratuitous violence that I will not have in my force of professional soldiers. I will be merciful, Sir, and not court martial you unless you insist upon making your presence known here. You may retain your rank if you leave the colonies at once."

"You will see no more of me here then, Sir. All the best fighting this damned insurgency without me." Grant stood up from his place at the table and stormed off.

"I say, General Howe, are you sure that was wise?" Gage remarked mildly. "He was a fairly competent officer."

"And a damned nuisance," Howe replied, "capable of poisoning the population against us with his rash behavior." "We will win this war by restoring the citizenry's esteem in us, not by terrorizing them. We are here to build bridges."

First Parish Unitarian Meeting House,
Medford, Massachusetts

July 4, 1775, 10:47 AM

General Henry Clinton was unable to compose himself. "Damme, General Howe, I must protest!" he said, pounding a fist on the table. "Your performance today was a far cry from the legends I have heard of from the front. Many a good man died in your ill-conceived assault! Tell me, General, was your late beloved brother no more skilled at battle than you?"

Finch sighed and sat back in his chair. The morning had been a difficult one. As the British army in Boston chased General Washington's army northwest, Howe's redcoats had quickly become the target of local Rebel partisans, who struck at the British flanks and rear as they passed. The Rebel skirmishers were quickly put to flight by the light infantry, but they were nevertheless able to harry the army's advance. Worse, when the Crown soldiers reached Medford Green, they found that the revolutionaries had erected a low wooden palisade to fend off the musketballs of the King.

It was against this wall, twice, that the Crown made a direct push by bayonet to drive the Rebels from the field. Howe had felt certain that the sight of the Crown forces would overwhelm the flagging morale of the Rebels and force them to surrender. But that did not occur. After a time, Howe, ordering Clinton to press the attack from the front, attempted to take the left flank of the Rebel position. But as his light infantry shifted their position, the Rebels, sensing danger, abandoned the field, fleeing southward. Before evacuating, however, Rebel fire had engulfed and shredded the King's men, leaving the Crown with a much-thinned line. When the smoke cleared, 308 soldiers lay dead; another 445 had been injured. For their part, the Rebels had 528 dead; 32 more, some wounded, were captured and sent back to Boston as prisoners of war.

Now the council had assembled in the First Parish Unitarian Meeting House in Medford. Reverend Ebenezer Turell, despite his allegedly Rebellious leanings, had offered his church to use as a field hospital. In the basement of the church, the gentlemen of war met, poring over maps.

Upon hearing Clinton's blustery rant, Finch held his breath, hoping that Howe would not meet the challenge Clinton had made. But, of course, Howe did. He glared across the table at Clinton and replied, his voice low, "Never...I repeat, NEVER talk to me of George again, General Clinton, do you hear? You may critique my battle tactics and stratagems, or even my own person, but speak to me so of my family and I shall have your hide, sir! Both of my brothers, be they Richard or George, were, are, and forever will be, better, stronger, and braver men than you."

Clinton's face turned red with rage, but he checked himself. "Yes, General Howe."

Howe stood and addressed his command. "I note a marked lack of esprit de corps in our ranks. We cannot let our differences destroy us. True, I faltered today, but I have learned from my errors. We must all do so, and we must work together."

Clinton nodded emphatically. "We're all very much aware of your feelings for the colonies, General Howe. They were your compatriots in the past war, by the wounds of God! But you must recognize that the men you fought alongside in the past war now seek to ruin us. We must win this war and preserve Britannia's might. If these colonies secede, why, who knows which territories will revolt next?"

"Quite!" Burgoyne said, drumming his fingers upon the table. "Think on it. We are protecting these Rebels from invasion by France or Spain. We are ensuring a better life for a populace that would be maltreated as captives, were we to let enemy nations conquer them."

"Indeed, General Burgoyne," Finch said. "There you have it. A new language, a new culture, likely new religious customs, and a whole new nation to which they would be forced to swear allegiance. We will save the colonies much trouble by protecting them from these matters, and more. You must also understand that these Rebels are hostile and vocal, yes, but a minority. Why, even according to the *Gazette*, they retain only a fifth of colonial sentiment. If we win the day more convincingly and visibly, they will be dissuaded from fighting us, and surely their numbers will dwindle."

"Gentlemen," Howe said firmly, "we shall break camp on the morrow and march southward after Mister Washington's army I have already taken care to dispatch dragoons to reconnoiter the terrain ahead, in the hope of finding advantageous ground." He sniffed. "Good day, sirs."

Southern Outskirts of Town, Cambridge, Massachusetts

July 5, 1775, 11:07 AM

Finch, Gage, and Clinton stood outside Howe's pavilion, ready to meet with General Howe as soon as he returned from the latrine. Finch held his spyglass in front of his chest, ready to pass it to his commanding officer.

Howe soon appeared, brushing off his uniform, and nodded brusquely to the waiting men. "Yes?"

Finch offered his spyglass to Howe, who took it and held it to his eye. Finch said, "They've left behind a rear guard, sir. Entrenched in Cambridge. These lads will probably put up a staunch defense whilst the rest of the Rebel army retreats. Truly, if we are to fight, we will pay in blood today. Yet if we do not, they shall find their way behind us and cause all manner of mischief."

"We shall see, Colonel," Howe replied, surveying the fields in the distance, then returning the spyglass to Finch. "Let us convene the council and discuss stratagems. Burgoyne should be back any moment now."

Howe's prediction proved correct. A few minutes later, with the thundering of hoofbeats, the red-coated dragoons began to appear over a nearby hill.

A quarter of an hour later, General Burgoyne rode up to the pavilion. He dismounted and bowed dramatically to the assembled company. "It appears, sir, that the enemy once more denies us the dignity of battle. The enemy's column is moving westward. The locals gossip that General Washington hopes to make a stand in Worcester, and I saw a small force, perhaps a regiment, providing a rearguard for his army in Cambridge. They likely hoped to ambush us in an intense street fight."

Howe nodded. "I see. We do not have nearly enough

horse to engage all the Rebels in a straight fight with cavalry alone." He turned to General Burgoyne. "But, General, were you to worry the enemy's main column and skirmish with the rearguard, I am sure the effect would be most desirable. It will allow us to challenge those men in town if they try to fall back alongside their allies. Meanwhile, a detachment of the men and I, and Finch here, will follow up with a frontal attack on Cambridge."

"Your servant, of course, sir," Burgoyne said, but there was worry in his eyes. "But would we not sustain horrific fire from the rear if the Rebel column were to wheel about?"

Howe nodded again. "It will be up to your discretion as to how long to hold your position behind the Rebel line. The column will be slow to reform if Washington decides to engage. And he may attempt to avoid a fight altogether."

Clinton glared at Howe. "I certainly hope you will not leave the rest of the army idle for this chance encounter, General Howe. What if some among the Rebel rearguard may be able to escape our horse – or, worse, overcome them? We should not leave our lights and grenadiers in reserve. A decisive victory is what we need to keep these Rebels in line and our men's spirits high. We should spare no expense. What say we close with Burgoyne's horse from behind, swinging wide between the Rebel column and rearguard, whilst you take your light bobs forward and close quickly with their front lines? The two forces would strike at roughly the same time, pinning the rearguard down.

Meanwhile, I shall lead a collection of line troops and grenadiers against one flank, while Governor Gage can lead a similar number of troops against the other. We may not end the conflict, but we would win a victory with few casualties, take a sizable town, and still have knowledge of where to pounce next."

Howe paused to consider this, then nodded once more.

Daniel H Lessin

"Perhaps a tad too prudent, but that is just the type of plan I favor. In doing so, we shall be sure to capture most of the rearguard."

"Perhaps not," Gage remarked, his brow furrowed in concern. "The retreating Rebels will recognize that their counterparts have fallen under attack and will be sure to return to render aid."

"At which point," Finch said, "our daring cavalry commander will run the gauntlet to safety. "If the Rebels deploy, we shall triumph in a straight fight even more convincingly. Is not the very reason they deployed a rearguard because they wished to distance themselves from our lines?"

"Quite so!" roared Clinton, pounding his fist on his thigh. "Now let us to battle!"

Cambridge Battlefield, Cambridge, Massachusetts
July 5, 1775, 12:02 PM

It was a glorious midsummer day as soldiers on both sides assembled for battle. The Charles River burbled nearby, and the smell of flowers filled the air. The King's men felt the sweaty heat of their wool coats as they awaited orders.

Howe addressed his men, squinting in the noonday sun. "Gentlemen, this is our time! We have trained long and hard for battle – though running down terrified farmers barely fits being called a battle. We shall triumph and conduct the colonies safely back to the bosom of His Majesty!"

Gage rallied his own men in a shaky but determined voice. "Now then, lads, the fight ahead will be for a just cause. Let us stay sharp, and minimize casualties for all, that God and decency and our King might prevail!"

At the same time, Clinton rallied his hatmen and

82

grenadiers. "All right, lads!" he cried, drawing a finger across his throat. "On my command, slit their gizzards! Give these scum a sound arse-kicking and the war will be won in no time at all!"

The British army moved steadily into position, waiting for the order to attack.

Then, as his light infantry approached the Rebel positions, Howe suddenly raised his hand, signaling a halt.

"Mister Cohen!" Howe shouted to the captain of the lights battalion. "I sense an opportunity." He scanned the buildings ahead of him, and a small smile crossed his lips. "A flag of truce, if you please. The rest of you, take a knee."

The lights looked at each other in surprise. Then they knelt and rested, waiting for their next order. Cohen stared at Howe in shock. A moment later, Finch realized that he was doing the same thing. He scanned the British forces. Clinton was scowling, his hands on his hips.

"Sir," Cohen replied, his voice filled with uncertainty. "No matter their numbers, we have more than enough men to take this town. Our soldiery will make short work of their militia. You need not worry."

Finch hurried over to Howe, fanning himself in the heat. "Do not forget as well, General Howe, that we are also hitting them from both flanks, and the rear as well, and—"

"The flag, Cohen," Howe repeated loudly.

Cohen reached into his pocket and drew out a white handkerchief.

"Wave it vigorously, Captain," Howe said firmly.

Cohen held up the makeshift flag and waved it back and forth beneath the becalmed sky.

Howe turned to Finch. "Well? Shall we pay them a visit?"

"Sir?" Finch replied. "Why are we offering to stand down?"

Howe smiled. "We have 2,000 men in full view, ready

to fight. The Rebels have perhaps 300. They cannot avoid recognizing our military superiority. Let us see if we can enable their surrender without bloodshed."

With Finch behind him, Howe strode with great ceremony toward the enemy position, a series of blockades along the King's Highway. Finch tried not to think about the hundreds of fowlers, muskets, and rifles pointed at them as they approached.

As they neared a green-shuttered brick house at the edge of one of the blockades, a nervous male voice shouted to them from its second-story window. "Stand back! What is it you want? You won't get through here without a fight!"

"Parley!" Howe shouted calmly, extending his two empty palms. "We do not seek battle. We merely wish to keep the peace. Rest your firelocks."

"Keep the peace!?" the voice shouted back. "Do you mean take us all prisoner rather than fight us?"

Howe held himself erect. "I do not, sir. I too would be as suspicious as you are, were I faced with your situation. But I beseech you – let me save your life. Stand forth with a staffer, Colonel. We are here to discuss terms, not to fight." Howe cleared his throat. "As we speak, your force is being surrounded by some of my best men, whilst your allies retreat in disorder. You are outnumbered almost ten to one, and we have the advantage of superior weaponry." He smiled. "There need not be bloodshed today, Colonel. Nobody wants it. If you were to disperse your corps, we would pass through town, and would not harm a soul unless confronted. If you truly care about the well-being of your people, why flood the streets with blood? You may keep your weapons, so long as you never again take up arms against the King."

The voice was silent for several seconds. Then it said, "Give me five minutes to decide my course of action."

"You may have them," Howe replied firmly.

Finch turned to the general and whispered to him, "Sir, you do realize that by dispersing the enemy without penalty, we offer them an opportunity to reconvene and face us on the battlefield again, later in the war?"

Howe smiled. "Perhaps. But our goal here is to restore the colonies to order. If we can do that with as little bloodshed and as much expedience as possible, so much the better for us all. If we treat them with respect, perhaps we might be paid the same honor."

A few minutes later, the door to the green-shuttered house opened, and a soldier stepped outside. Then he stopped and stood to attention. He was dressed in full regalia, including a brown coat with epaulettes and a red sash around his waist, where a saber was anchored. A staffer stood behind him.

Drawing his blade, the colonel mutely saluted General Howe. Then the two stepped forward together. "Joseph Gist, sir, at your service," the colonel said icily.

Howe bowed slightly. "William Howe, at yours. You will accept our terms?"

Gist gestured toward the Rebel soldiers. "These are good men. I cannot throw their lives away. But I require your word of honor that there will be no attacks, no searches, no arrests, and no confiscation of weapons or powder."

"You have that word," Howe said earnestly. "I understand your concern. Everyone shall be treated with the utmost respect. Furthermore, I shall communicate your colony's grievances to our King. Many of those grievances are not without merit."

Gist removed his saber and presented it to Howe, handle first. Howe accepted it with a solemn nod. Then he smiled and loudly addressed the Rebel troops.

"Gentlemen, I stand before you impressed. You were well positioned to give us a good run of it and to cost us dearly in combat. However, today we will both prevail. Colonel Gist and I hereby disperse you, with honor and appreciation for your bravery and hard work. Take care and may God go with you and with us."

A minute later, under Gist's orders, the Rebels dispersed in full ceremony. They marched down the lane past the shuttered houses of brick and wood, their weapons at hand but unused. The redcoats followed close behind, watching for any sort of hostility, but finding none.

As they entered the town of Cambridge, Finch could barely fathom this uncanny, peaceable victory. Better yet, this resolution would build esteem for the British army in the eyes of many colonials. Finch found the situation awkward but gratifying.

The Cap and Cloak Inn, Cambridge, Massachusetts
July 5, 1775, 5:48 PM

That evening, at Howe's order, his command dined in one of the local public houses with Gist and two of his captains. The atmosphere was tense, and all of the other patrons stared shamelessly at the group. At first, the Rebel leaders stammered a little when Howe engaged them in polite conversation. After a few minutes, however, their words flowed more freely – though they seemed loath to discuss the war.

"It's a dark time in our nation when brother turns against brother," Gist said finally. "I want nothing more of it, and really wanted little of it to begin with, but was shamed into fighting by my high standing in town. I'm the foremost clothier in all Cambridge, you see."

"An enviable title," Finch replied, regarding the uniforms of some of his soldiers. "I suppose that is why all your men are so well dressed."

"Indeed," came the reply of militia Captain Benjamin Hawkins. "Personally, I'm a naturalist, but we are all volunteers who came to the protection of our people. We do not bear King George any ill will, but his parliament seeks to tax us without our proper representation in parliament. Though a minor infraction, we fear for what might come next. Please convey our respects to His Majesty and help him understand our plight."

Howe said, "I acknowledge your perspective and shall certainly send word to the King. This is provided that you also spread word of our understanding of the situation." He gazed around the table, then around the room. "We do not mean you gentlemen, nor your wives and children, any harm. But I must remind you that you benefitted heavily from our protection in the late war with the French. This, and for no other reason, is why parliament felt a need to tax you. And while His Majesty may have indeed levied duties upon you lightly and provisionally after the conflict for this assistance, he taxed the home country all the more – not only in far greater duties paid to the Crown, but in blood, fighting France and Her allies the world over. Let not a miniscule tax turn you away from us."

That evening, both inside and outside the public house, redcoat dined with minuteman.

As dusk approached, the British forces, at Gist's invitation, set up camp on the outskirts of Cambridge. Rebels, Loyalists, and Crown soldiers spent a few peaceful hours singing songs, swapping stories, and wishing each other a swift end to the conflict.

The next morning, the King's men paraded through town, unharmed and unopposed. Finch caught sight of Clinton, who slowly ambled along Brattle Street upon his horse, eyes downcast.

"General Clinton!" Finch shouted. "Good morning to you!"

Clinton looked up, his expression surprisingly subdued. "Finch. Good morning. What a turn of events, eh? Howe did a good job, loath as I am to say it. It is wondrous to know that some of us military men excel at matters other than killing. And what a waste killing is. Keeps a man from hearth, home, and family, sir. All I wish is to reunite with my children, now that my wife has passed. Married only five years. Can you believe the tragedy, sir?"

"My sympathies," replied Finch. "My own wife has recently evacuated Boston with my children. Already do I miss them, especially since I hear so many tales of soldiers taking their families on the campaign trail."

"You have hit upon it exactly!" Clinton exclaimed. "My advice to you is to never leave your family again, if possible. A lesson I learned myself too late. I still yearn for their presence. They would be a boon in wartime, not a burden."

"Precisely," Finch said. "Had she not been born a woman, my wife Adelaide would likely have been at the front herself, so fierce and proud is she! And my young Caroline rides like one of General Burgoyne's best."

Clinton laughed. "I am sure we could have used her."

The Cap and Cloak Inn, Cambridge, Massachusetts
July 6, 1775, 10:06 AM

Finch captured Clinton's rook with another ambitious maneuver by his queen. "General Clinton, you are not focusing on the game. Please concentrate. Your men are falling in droves."

Finch and Clinton were playing chess at the Cap and

Cloak Inn. Though they were both in good spirits, Clinton was loudly arguing the case for the forced abolition of African slavery in the colonies.

"By God, sir! We'll free the slaves, rally the abolitionists to our side, and seize the moral high ground from those conniving Rebels. We'll expose them for the hypocrites they are, damn them! Liberty and justice, my arse!"

"One step at a time, my friend," Finch replied. "Surely we must win this war first. We cannot succeed without Loyalists, many of whom also own black laborers. Justice will prevail; just give it time."

Clinton began to respond, but was interrupted by the arrival of a breathless messenger. "Sirs! General Howe requests your presence in the chapel basement of the college."

"Thank you," Clinton growled. He turned to Finch. "Another topic for another day, my friend. But, one of these days, these injustices will be righted, even if I must right them myself."

The two set off toward the chapel. As they passed by some Loyalist provincials undergoing training exercises, Clinton shouted a brief encouragement and waved at them. The Loyalists stiffly poised their firelocks in return.

"They're getting better, aren't they, Finch?" Clinton observed with a grin.

Holden Chapel, Harvard College,
Cambridge, Massachusetts

July 6, 1775, 10:14 AM

Clinton and Finch cautiously walked down the dimly lit steps to the basement of Holden Chapel. They found themselves brushing past spider webs and bracing against bookshelves that overflowed with dusty religious texts.

In the room at the bottom, illuminated by lanterns, were Howe, Gage, and Burgoyne, impatiently waiting for them.

Howe's eyes narrowed as they entered. "Clinton. Finch. Good of you to grace us with your presence. Now sit."

Finch and Clinton silently perched themselves on two battered stools.

"Gentlemen," Howe said grimly. "The colonists have instigated the unthinkable. We have a full-scale rebellion upon our hands."

The others groaned.

"A rash of skirmishes have abounded in Virginia, Georgia, North Carolina, and New York. Lord Dunmore has engaged in combat with the enemy, and many of our other Royal governors have fled their posts. While Loyalist militias are forming, it is my reluctant duty to inform you that we now have a far greater expanse of land over which to fight for the safety of our people." Howe paused and looked at each of his commanders, one by one. "To make matters still worse, I have received word from Governor Carleton that Fort Ticonderoga is missing a collection of siege guns. They were evidently captured by the Rebellion sometime before his arrival." Howe sighed. "Though Sir Guy has retaken the fort, we may yet have quite the fight in our future."

"Very well, then, sir," Finch said. "We have a revolution on our hands, not to mention a civil war for the poor souls of the continent who choose to follow us into battle. We are at your disposal. Is there a new course of action to be followed?"

Howe shook his head. "Not for us. I believe my stratagems remain sound. Prevost and Haldimand will see to our southern front; we have the northern front. Our two armies will secure their respective regions and reinforce the garrisons of the large towns as we go. For ourselves, we shall begin by marching westward, attempting to engage Washington's forces if and when we can. All the while, we shall detach elements to occupy such important towns as Hartford, Connecticut and Springfield, Massachusetts. Another, smaller force will be detached to occupy New Hampshire and Northern Massachusetts. Then we will swing around and assist in liberating whatever of Rhode Island remains in Rebel hands after Pitcairn has had his say."

Howe stood up, a deep frown on his face. "The Rebels will truly be out for blood. May God save the King, his colonies, and our mortal souls."

Five hours later, the King's army marched through and out of Cambridge, passing peacefully into the countryside. The soldiers fell into a slow march as the fifes and drums played "Scipio."

chapter 5.

A Jaunt to Newport

November 17, 1775, 2:02 PM

After many months of giving chase to General George Washington's so-called patriots, things appeared to be going well for the British Army under General William Howe. At long last, the Crown forces stationed in New England had pushed the Rebellion's Continental Army from Massachusetts, as well as from northeastern New York and New Hampshire. Small Crown detachments, backed by newly trained Loyalist provincials, were also pushing into Connecticut and Rhode Island. Though spy rings and partisans kept both Loyalists and Rebels on their toes, battles between both sides' northern armies were few and far between, and martial law kept the colonies largely in tow. In Boston, the streets were as peaceful as could be hoped for, and Finch settled in for what he hoped would be an uneventful winter.

An early snow fell in New England, bringing an end to the fighting for a time. Law and order persisted in Boston, but this did not dampen the local children's spirits as they dashed amid the flakes. They mingled freely with the British soldiers, some jovially falling into marching order alongside detachments of the Crown forces. Others pelted the soldiers with snowballs, sometimes in jest, sometimes with more hostility.

For a few short months, Finch could relax. For now, he was away from the endless marching, the restless nights attempting to sleep under canvas, and the inconclusive conflict. He knew that there would be more fighting before the rebellion could be quashed, but he hoped that the winter would be a time of respite.

Yet, it was not to be. Finch's conscience refused to leave him alone after a letter from Adelaide was slipped underneath his door in the guest quarters of Governor Gage's mansion. He read it with a combination of delight, yearning, and guilt.

September 3rd 1775

Dear Husband,

How kind of you to think of me at last, despite the onus of military labor weighing upon your shoulders. The children and I, along with your hound, fare just fine, thank you. We have settled into your family home, as our duty commands us. Jacob has been a model host, and has amused us well with stories of your youth alongside him, and the various adventures the two of you had. He bids me remind you of one "Yorkshire pudding incident," truly an entertaining tale.

And yet, despite these distractions, how the children miss their father, asking after reports of your entanglements. They are rightfully upset with the dearth of letters sent to us and are as inquisitive about your adventures as you are of theirs.

Caroline has come to enjoy energetic interaction with stable boys, who have provided her with the continued opportunity to ride like the wind, whilst Constance has tended to spend more time alongside myself in attending parties for the families of soldiery here in Chelmsford. It is an idyllic place, but we have yet to truly enjoy it, as we are missing a significant component of our family.

Still, we attempt to make do. Caroline has already attempted to run off to Bristol and befriend the sailors more than once. Archibald continues to search for inspiration, but stays close by his mother, and some are beginning to whisper about his future. Finally, though he misses his master, Gus sends his regards and seems to have, at length, settled into life without you. I am sure he would take great joy in your return, however, as would we all.

For all the joys of the autumn and the beauteous foliage therewith, I must admit that, though I continue to be wroth with your decision, I miss you greatly. Where is my romantic poet? My deliciously awkward engineer who showered me with affection? I daresay the mistake was mine for not pursuing a more aggressive course in staying in Boston, but Lieutenant Colonel Rattigan's esteemed protégé should have fought harder to keep me on site as well.

With love, and only hoping you return it to me one of these days, lest the international incident we nearly caused as ambitious young engineer and cunning handmaiden in King Frederick's ballroom be forgot!
    Your beloved wife,
    Adelaide

Finch's remorse harried him for the next two days, until he received a letter from General Howe that somewhat improved matters – and his spirits.

To the Esteemed Colonel Finch,

Your services have been greatly appreciated in my army, and I should think that without them, the presence of the Crown in these thirteen colonies would be much diminished.

As the winter takes hold over the colonies, I charge you to travel to Newport, in the colony of Rhode Island, to reinforce the garrison of John Pitcairn, who has since occupied the town and received Virginia's governor, John Murray, the Lord Dunmore. There, you will supervise the building of fortifications to protect the colony from recapture by the forces of the rebellion.

    W. Howe

At last, here was an opportunity to be far away from the endless drama and quarrels, and to do what he was trained to do.

Finch immediately began packing, eager to set off and begin work on the project.

He arranged to be taken, along with his possessions, in an ox-drawn wagon driven by a young local boy named Adrian. They were escorted by two mounted dragoons – a taciturn, pencil-thin man named Watson, and an enormous, loquacious, and surprisingly intelligent man named Grimme, who seemed to squash his horse underneath him with his great girth.

Together, the two solemnly escorted the cart. All four wore plainclothes so as not to be detected by revolutionaries intent on attacking British troops. Although Finch was slightly nervous about the possibility of a Rebel ambush, he also knew that few people in their right minds would travel this distance in the cold of winter.

It was a long journey, and the expedition's progress was

slow. Partly to pass the time, Finch often put pen to paper and created a few initial sketches for the fort.

The night after Finch and his party reached Providence, however, the party was met with a surprise. Just as Finch was falling asleep in the Inn of the Waxing Moon, flanked on either side by the dragoons, and with Adrian on a quilt on the floor, they were roused by a series of fowler shots outside.

Grimme quickly threw himself on top of Finch, nearly suffocating him. Watson rose and left the room to investigate, pistol in hand. Finch pushed Grimme away, rolled out of bed, and crouched cautiously behind it.

A stressful, quiet minute passed. Then another, then several more.

Eventually, Watson returned, still brandishing his pistol, a pair of ruffians in tow.

"I tell you again, *sir!*" slurred one young man, obviously drunk. "We were just celebrating the arrival of Crown operatives!"

"So you reveal our presence?" Watson growled. "You have given away our position. Now we must displace again."

"As you would have it, sir. We just wanted to celebrate your passing by. You won't find too many of us Loyalists here in Providence. Most of us are staunchly Rebellious. Like my wife and children and all my other relatives."

Grimme loomed over the two young men. "Tell us how you gleaned our identities. Now."

The other ruffian spoke. "Your clothing, sir. You look like a bunch of slack-jawed yokels. Providence is a sophisticated city where we know how to properly attire ourselves. We knew at once that you are not from here – and that one or more of you are likely British officers travelling in disguise."

Finch sighed. "All right," he said to Grimme. "Begin packing. We'll leave here as quickly as possible."

Half an hour later, the four set off again, taking the road toward Newport.

Late that morning, with Finch frequently dozing off in the wagon, they made it to the outskirts of Providence. There, on the riverbank, a ferryman sat idly on his flat-bottomed boat, his pole resting beside him.

"Good morning, lads," the ferryman greeted them. "Five pounds each. And five more for the animals and cart."

Finch's eyebrows shot up. "Sir! Twenty-five pounds for a single crossing? That is a greatly excessive sum of money. I do not know if you understand to whom you speak, but we are not fools to be taken advantage of. The Crown would not stand to hear of this highway robbery."

"Two pounds overall," Watson said. "Not a penny more."

"Now then, sir," the ferryman replied calmly. "I know not if you are a man of commerce, but internal conflict deals providers like me a harsh blow. These are challenging times for us all, and so I must enact a wartime duty. You British surely understand the need to tax. I've got a family and the Crown is tearing them apart."

"And yet, we're here to protect those families," Finch said sternly, "Mister—"

"Andrews," the ferryman finished for him. He spoke very loudly, so that the few locals on the road could hear. "And I certainly appreciate that, indeed I do. But to fleece an old man like me of his livelihood in a time of conflict should be a war crime in itself. Your man here should be shot for suggesting such a low price, he should!"

To Finch's surprise, Adrian stepped forward. "Our price was fair! It was yours that was obscene. I've known many ferrymen to take far less as a fee. Take us across, sir, for the reasonable price of two pounds."

The Ferryman frowned. "I do not know what possesses your friends to charge so little, boy, but in this case, I shall be lenient. Though the winds are strong and the water is choppy – and though one of your men is the size of a cow – I can take all of you for 15 pounds."

There was a moment of tense silence.

"Five pounds," Watson said finally.

Andrews sighed dramatically. "Very well. You're lucky that business is slow today. Climb aboard."

The ferryman guided them onto his craft. Though the waters were as choppy as he claimed, he knew his trade well. Waves lapped at the ferry throughout the crossing, but he was able to convey them to Newport with relative ease.

As Finch and his party climbed slowly out of the boat onto the dock, Andrews smiled at a large family waiting expectantly nearby.

"Good day!" he shouted. "I presume you are looking for transportation to Providence? I shall take you there at once. Five pennies each."

The Crown and Anchor Pub, Newport, Rhode Island

Sunday, November 19, 1775, 8:17 PM

Newport, like Boston, was a sizable, well-developed town. Though the gusty winter air blew throughout, it appeared to barely give the hardy citizens pause as they went about their activities. Finch drew his watchcoat close around himself, wondering how they managed it, day after day.

After some exploration of the town, Finch found lodging in a tiny, dingy inn. He put his belongings in his room, then hurried to the pub downstairs to order a late dinner.

As he was finishing a meal of some sausage and turnips, he heard a distinctive voice behind him.

"Finch? Is that you, my good man?"

Finch turned. Standing in the doorway was Major Pitcairn. He looked tired and had great circles under his eyes, but his delight at seeing Finch again seemed genuine. Finch stood and the two embraced. "Sir Marine, have I stories for you!" Finch announced. "Please, have a seat."

The two spent the next half hour entertaining each other with tales of war.

"Though we seem to be winning individual battles," Finch told Pitcairn over a plate of baked beans, "no end to the fighting is in sight. What's more, some of our commanders hate each other. Clinton is finally growing to respect Howe. But he cannot stand Burgoyne and recognizes that he is something of a fop. Meanwhile, Burgoyne despises Clinton's joyless nature. Howe is angry at both of them for fighting with each other. It's a right circus out there! I'm glad to be in the relative safety of Newport, away from all of them."

Pitcairn smiled sadly. "Goodness, sir, but that is something! Alas, such is the way of things. Rarely in war can you choose your allies, no matter how it seems. Fortunately, I have a tale to tell that is not nearly so depressing."

Finch nodded. "Go on."

Pitcairn leaned forward. "As we made our march from Boston toward Newport, the Rebels decided to ambush us as we crossed through Providence. My men, though forced into a desperate defensive action, fared well for themselves against the initial attacks, repelling two assaults from the protection of the town with the assistance of the Royal Navy. But in the days that followed, we watched in distress as the Rebel numbers grew. At length, just when matters were looking particularly grim, we happened upon a plan. In addition to enlisting the aid of the local Loyalists, doubling our numbers, we quickly and covertly purchased some clothes from local merchants. Then we of the marines began marching ourselves up and down the square, sometimes in civilian attire alongside our new allies, sometimes in our marine uniforms, to make it seem as though our Crown numbers, which began with just a few British marines, had been tripled. This gave the Rebels pause. Rather than storm our position, they attempted to starve us out. But after only a few days, Lord Dunmore arrived with his men. Between all of us, we enveloped them and forced their surrender. A damned fine achievement, if I may say so myself. Dunmore and his men conducted themselves admirably."

"Ha!" Finch said. "Well done. It seems that, under your command, I shall be quite safe and relaxed in my labors." He paused. "Tell me, is there anything at all I should be wary of here in Newport?"

Pitcairn nodded thoughtfully. "Apart from the dangers of the Sons of Liberty, the potential threats are twofold. First, there is Lord Dunmore himself. He has views that some feel are scandalous. I fear not the views themselves, so much as how far he takes them. The man is careless and impulsive. However, he may wreak a horrible vengeance against us if we question his authority as governor of Virginia and commander of over 700 soldiers. In addition, we do not know how His Majesty feels about Dunmore."

"Understood," Finch said. "A crazed governor who does not know his limits and may or may not have royal backing. Anything else?"

"Yes. Lord Dunmore's soldiers. They have been a constant thorn in our backside. Lord Dunmore does not control his troops very well. Thus it was Governor Wanton's decision to billet only Dunmore's white soldiers – perhaps 400 of the Queen's Own Loyal Virginians – in town. As for the African soldiers, the governor has confined all 300 or so to the ships they sailed in on. They made for dangerous and undisciplined interactions, worrying my patrols and brawling with civilians, Loyalist and Rebel alike. Avoid them if you can."

November 20, 1775, 3:32 PM

Finch stood stiffly in the center of Governor Wanton's sitting room. It was cold and sterile, with high cross-vaults and a tiled floor. In front of him, alone at a small table, sat Lord Dunmore. He was reading the newspaper and half ignoring Finch.

"Your Grace? Lord Dunmore?"

Silence. Dunmore continued reading.

"Sir, it is about your African soldiers," Finch said.

After a few seconds, the governor rolled his eyes. Still looking at his newspaper, he sighed and spoke in a Scottish brogue. "What would you have me do, Colonel? I realize my Ethiopian warriors ran amok, brawling and cursing, so I let His Majesty's well-trained forces billet them in our ships. Let the Crown teach them some discipline." He cleared his throat. "I hereby donate them to the British army. Send in Pitcairn's marines to restore order among them. Just do not re-enslave them. I promised them their freedom, and imprisoning them would prove me a liar."

Finch cleared his own throat. "No doubt, Governor," he replied. "But we can reasonably expect you to take responsibility for your men. We are grateful that you have brought so many into the service of the Crown, and thus far they have fought bravely and well. But as they are under your command, it is your duty to both provide for them and control them."

The governor raised a contemptuous eyebrow and, at last, turned his gaze on Finch. "I do not care to command a regiment. I was merely looking out for the best interests of Virginia. Now that these men are here, many of them newly free from the bonds of enslavement, they should be subject to the decisions and powers of the local authorities."

Finch stood tall. "Governor Murray, I have leave from General Howe to lock you up at my discretion for creating widespread disorder. Are you sure you do not wish to follow my suggestions and accept your responsibility for your men?"

Dunmore dropped his newspaper. "Such cheek! How dare you, a colonel, question a governor!"

"On military matters, and when simply bearing news from a higher command, I see no reason why I should not, sir."

Lord Dunmore glared at Finch. "And what, exactly, is my transgression? Delivering to General Howe and Major Pitcairn two regiments of soldiers – soldiers who promptly helped to push back Rebel attacks?"

Finch glared back. "General Henry Clinton made it amply clear to me that he will happily take command of your black soldiers, along with the Queen's Own Loyal Virginians, and provide for all of them." Finch took a long breath. "So, Lord Dunmore, your arrest will likely improve the conditions of the former slaves. We are giving you one last opportunity to do your duty for His Majesty. I will help you, if you like."

Lord Dunmore sighed. For several seconds, he sat in silence. Finally, he remarked grimly, "It was not until I took up the mantle of Virginia's governor that I met such disagreeable people as you and Howe. Very well, then, Finch. I shall address the freemen aboard my ship at 6:00 p.m. tonight. You shall be there with me. Until then, I will spread the word and order my fellow Virginians to be present."

Newport Docks, Newport, Rhode Island

November 24, 1775, 5:50 PM

Lord Dunmore tipped his hat to passing workers as he and Finch stepped onto the Newport docks. "Have you planned your speech fully, Lord Dunmore?" Finch inquired of him.

"My mind is an ingenious instrument," Dunmore replied. He pointed to his brain. "Everything I need to deliver my speech is up here."

The two stepped into a small rowboat that was waiting for them. They took their seats, and a minute later, the harbor pilot guided them toward a collection of ships anchored off the port in town. It was there that the HMS *Fowey*, Lord Dunmore's personal frigate, awaited them.

Both Finch and the Virginian governor were quiet as they approached the small fleet. Finch wondered how he had somehow become Lord Dunmore's lackey, tending to his every need. Beside him, Lord Dunmore muttered words and phrases to himself, apparently preparing his address to his men in his head. Finch drew his watchcoat tight as cold winter air gusted over the bow.

There was great rejoicing amongst the black soldiers aboard the ships as the tender containing Lord Dunmore and Finch was hoisted onto the frigate. Lord Dunmore grinned at them confidently, and for the next several minutes he strode up and down the deck, rubbing his hands and speaking a few words here and there to individual men. Finch followed behind him, doing his best to gauge the soldiers' condition. Some stood firmly at attention, but more slouched, having clearly taken ill. Some of the men appeared poxy; others hacked, coughed, and sneezed. Several reeked of fish and turned bowels.

Lord Dunmore finished his greetings and mounted the

staircase to the poop deck. Finch followed, feeling a mix of pity, disgust, dread, and curiosity.

For at least another half minute, Lord Dunmore silently surveyed the assembled men, grinning hugely. Finally, he cleared his throat and began to speak.

"Ethiopian Regiment! Hear me! As I promised you, I have freed you from bondage and led you on a great voyage to the promised land of Newport! Here you stand – free men in the protection of the Crown."

Some of the men stared questioningly at Dunmore, but there was also some ragged whooping and hollering, as well as much hacking and coughing.

Lord Dunmore smiled at their response, then sliced the sky with his hand to call for silence. He spoke again. "Free though you are, I feel my work is not yet done. All is not well here."

"Is that not obvious?" a black soldier shouted.

Finch had to turn away and cover his mouth to hide a snicker.

The soldier continued: "We're sick as dogs and unwelcome in your promised land of emancipation. Meanwhile a war is on, and there is a bounty out for our heads. If we're caught, we'd be lucky to be killed mercifully. We will more likely be forced to work the fields once more."

Dunmore raised an eyebrow and trained his gaze on the soldier.

"Too right, of course, Mister…"

"I don't have a family name," the soldier replied gruffly. "My name is Duke."

"Well, then, Sir Duke," Dunmore said. Suddenly, he clapped Finch on the shoulder and pulled him forward. "We fortunately have a war hero among us. Using Mister Finch's influence over our beloved governor of Rhode Island, tomorrow he will conduct us all into the city with a smile.

There you will be fed, housed, treated for all your maladies, and rehabilitated. Thereafter, we shall use Newport as our base of operations to bring freedom to all slaves."

"Both Loyalist and Rebel-owned?" another freedman shouted out.

To Finch's amazement, Dunmore paused and thought on it, then turned to him. "Well, what do you think, Finch?"

"Lord Dunmore, I—"

"There's a good lad! Finch, address the Crown's finest regiment from Virginia, would you, please?" Dunmore took two quick steps backward, leaving Finch standing alone before the crowd.

Finch swallowed hard, his head spinning. He began speaking, with no idea what he was about to say. "Men of Virginia," he said. "As I stand here—"

A shout interrupted him. "York here," the voice said. "Former slave to Mister Patrick Henry. I take it, then, that this means we're allowed to mete out our own justice against our former masters?"

Finch blanched. "Well, that's not exactly the point of the British legal system—"

Dunmore stepped to Finch's side and interrupted him. "What Finch means to say is that you can rest assured that slave owners, at least the Rebel ones, will be punished. Meanwhile, you are free men and, as soldiers in His Majesty's army, will have the opportunity and the gratification of releasing others from bondage."

There were a few scattered cheers, along with an equal number of cries of derision.

Dunmore suddenly stood tall and straight. "What we all must focus on is that, together, we're going to defeat the Rebels and free all slaves. That includes the ones here in Rhode Island, the ones in Virginia, and so many others besides." He began gesturing furiously with both hands. "One day we shall let freedom reign across all these lands. For the black man, the white man, and the native. That day will come once the war is won!"

That brought a huge, sudden roar of approval and a scattered clapping of hands. Lord Dunmore basked in the approval for several seconds. Then he turned to Finch.

"This is how you win a war," he said softly, and winked. Then he raised both his fists and smiled smugly.

Joseph Wanton's Mansion, Newport, Rhode Island
November 25, 1775, 10:04 AM

Finch waited once again in the sitting room of the Rhode Island governor's mansion, his gut filled with dread, preparing himself for the dialogue to come.

A footman appeared and announced, "The governor will see you now, Colonel Finch."

Finch wordlessly nodded his thanks and stood up. As he began walking alongside the servant, he felt his hands shaking.

The footman ushered Finch into Wanton's office and quickly retreated.

Governor Joseph Wanton was a tall, bespectacled man with a wiry frame. He stood next to a polished wooden desk on which there was a tall stack of papers. He looked at Finch with curiosity, then spoke with great eloquence and poise. "Ah, yes, our new engineer. Mister Finch. Sit down, please." It was both an invitation and an order.

Finch sat in one of the two horsehair chairs in front of the desk.

"I understand you have a complaint about John Murray and his blackamoors," Wanton said. "Damned nuisance they are, crowding up my port."

"Yes, governor," Finch said slowly. "I agree that they do not belong on the ships."

Wanton shook his head. His face showed a flicker of annoyance. "But they do, Mister Finch. On the ships. Not on my docks. You have some military authority, do you not? Would you kindly ensure they stay on their vessels, that they might ride out the winter there?"

Finch coughed. "Actually, sir, I was a little surprised to see that they have not been billeted in the barracks provided for soldiers, alongside their white comrades. They are, after all, soldiers themselves."

Wanton briefly pursed his lips. "They are ill, sir, are they not?"

"Some of them. According to Lord Dunmore, many have fevers from being outdoors all day in the cold weather after a long sea journey."

"Perils of military service, I suppose," Governor Wanton replied. "I do believe our fellows in the Queen's Own Loyal Virginians fared no better."

Finch raised an eyebrow. "Perhaps, sir. Nevertheless, we have men dying from preventable diseases. I respectfully request that we billet them at once in houses, like their fellow white soldiers from Virginia."

One of Wanton's eyelids flickered. "And yet, Mister Finch, consider their background. These Ethiopians of Lord Dunmore's have proven to be rowdy and poorly behaved. I do not feel comfortable risking their presence within my city until they can comport themselves like gentlemen."

Finch barely restrained himself from raising his voice. "Contempt for rulership knows no race, Governor Wanton. Surely the Rebels have demonstrated that. Governor Murray and I have spoken to his soldiers, sir. They are sure to be more respectful now."

Wanton snorted. "Their very presence causes my

people to become ill at ease. Do you seriously feel that a quick speech can inspire them to change their natures?" Finch looked at Wanton stonily. "When that speech comes from Lord Dunmore, yes. He is their leader and commander."

Wanton met Finch's gaze, and the two stared each other down for several seconds.

Then footfalls heralded the return of the governor's servant. He knocked and entered, carrying himself with the utmost poise. "Governor Wanton? Admiral Howe requests your audience."

Wanton did not acknowledge his servant. Instead, he scowled at Finch. "I believe we are done discussing the matter, Colonel Finch. However, I understand you have yet to meet the admiral. Attend here a moment. Perhaps you may wish to complain about my conduct to him." He glanced briefly at the footman. "Show the admiral in."

A moment later, Admiral Howe stepped into the room. He was a hefty man, well dressed in blue with gold lace. His round, bewigged face bore a tragic expression as he briefly wiped his brow. He nodded to Finch, then turned to Wanton.

Governor Wanton smiled broadly. "Ahoy there, Admiral Howe!" Wanton said. "How go preparations for the docking of the fleet for the winter?"

"Passing well, Governor Wanton. I foresee no problems for what I hope will be a mild season." Howe scowled deeply. "But I still see that we have some 300 refugees from Lord Dunmore's expedition to offload. I do not understand why so many sickly, idle blackamoors have yet to make landfall."

Finch suddenly had an idea. Turning to Howe, he affected an apologetic expression.

"Those are not mere refugees, Admiral Howe, but Lord Dunmore's soldiers. You have opined, have you not, as to the merit of the Negro sailor? That your West Indians stood as good a man as any in your fleet? Well, Lord Dunmore seems to agree with you. And so do I."

Howe was taken aback. "Soldiers? Why are they not billeted with the marines and other Royalists, then?"

Finch grinned. "Why, indeed? How could I be so thoughtless? My deepest apologies, Admiral. Governor Wanton, might I perchance erect makeshift barracks in town for these valiant soldiers, who have come all this way to fight by our side?"

The governor rolled his eyes, then shook his head and grimaced at the engineer. "Finch…"

Howe looked hard at Wanton. "Governor Wanton, surely you haven't told Finch to not house these poor wretches? How can we expect them to fight for us if we don't treat them like soldiers?"

The governor shook his head again. "Very well," he said grimly. "Finch, you may proceed."

Finch saluted Admiral Howe. "I shall get to work at once on those barracks."

"What about the fort?" Wanton asked nervously.

"In time, sir!" Finch replied.

Howe laughed. "But in sooth, Governor," he said. "Who needs a fort so urgently when we have a wall of ships standing by?"

chapter 6.
Onward to Hartford

Governor Wanton's Mansion, Newport, Rhode Island
February 12, 1776, 8:04 AM

Finch yawned luxuriously as he surveyed his surroundings. His room, one of the many guest rooms in Governor Wanton's mansion, was well furnished. It had an enormous desk, which for weeks he had covered with drawings for the new fort.

That fort had been completed nearly a month ago. Now Finch's sea chest stood at the ready, prepared to convey his personal belongings at a moment's notice. His four-poster bed afforded him great comfort in his sleep. The room's full-length mirror allowed him to bemoan his portly physique.

The room also had a grand fireplace, an elaborate carpet, and several wall hangings. Finch felt quite well insulated from the outdoors, which today looked especially frigid and snowy.

"Urgent message for Colonel Finch!" came a cry from

111

outside his door. A moment later there was a loud knock on the door as well.

Finch groaned. He hoped this was not about Lord Dunmore's men again.

"Who goes?"

"A message from Colonel Richard Prescott, sir. He asks that you and your soldiers march on New London at once to reinforce his pursuit of General Washington's column."

Finch froze. The request seemed odd and unlikely. "As you say, sir, but have you any documentation to confirm this endeavor? It strikes me as strange that—"

"Of course!" said the voice through the door. There was some rustling, and a dispatch was pushed underneath.

Finch picked it up, broke the seal, withdrew a note, and began reading.

February 1, 1776

To Colonel Giles Finch.

As we have reported in past dispatches, Governor Sir Guy Carleton and I marched many miles from Mount Royal and have retaken Fort Ticonderoga from the Rebel hordes, then marched on Albany, where we won another resounding victory. We now march south in pursuit of the corps of George Washington, who seems headed toward the town of New London, in the colony of Connecticut, where there is a Rebel stronghold of indeterminate size. We will take on supplies in Hartford and march on New London, where we shall presumably do battle. We desire any reinforcements that you could furnish as soon as possible, that we may put an end to this noxious rebellion.

With regards, I remain your obedient servant, &c.
  R. Prescott

Finch took a moment to gather himself. This seemed to agitate the messenger on the other side of the door, who spoke with great urgency. "Colonel Prescott requires your immediate reply, sir. My orders are to collect your answer and deliver it to him as swiftly as possible."

Finch contemplated the situation. If the Crown forces were to finally deal Washington and his column a decisive defeat, the cause of Rebellion would suffer a crushing blow.

What's more, a superior officer had commanded *him*, Giles Finch, to cut off the enemy.

Finch opened the door. The messenger stood waiting, ready to run a return dispatch to Colonel Prescott. He looked to be about 14 years of age. He had mossy teeth and a hunched posture.

"Very well, young man. You have my attention. Let me find a pen and ink."

Governor Wanton's Mansion, Newport, Rhode Island

February 12, 1776, 11:40 AM

The idea of rousing hundreds of soldiers for a winter campaign, it turned out, was not well received. Admiral Howe, the commanding officer in town, was especially displeased.

"I won't command you to stay put, Finch," Admiral Howe said when Finch showed him the letter, "but I would have certainly preferred it if we had direct orders from my brother allowing for it."

"I understand, sir. So, may I order a regiment of soldiers to accompany me?"

"This is highly irregular, Finch. I won't be held responsible if my brother grows angry at you."

"And angry he may be, sir," Finch replied, "but I shall

take full responsibility for my activity in the decisions at hand. Allow me to suggest that I take only the Ethiopian Regiment on this campaign. They are not popular among the locals, they are eager to fight, and they need to gain battle experience."

Howe pondered the idea for several seconds. Finally, he shook his head sadly and said, "If you want those men, you may have them under three conditions. First, you will need approval from Governor Murray himself. Second, you will equip them only with what powder they had to begin with, and nothing more. We will not waste our good powder on this jaunt. Third, we have no orders to march to Connecticut, so the marines will not accompany you. The local Loyalists are unlikely to join you as well. If these are terms under which you are willing to march west, then I will not stop you."

"Thank you, sir."

As soon as Finch left the governor's mansion, he set out to find Pitcairn. Surely Pitcairn might be willing to lend a *few* marines to the fight. *Perhaps*, Finch thought, *the marines might even help train the Ethiopians into a more effective force.*

After an hour's search, Finch finally located the major in the officers' mess, talking and joking with one of his ensigns, Rothwald.

As Finch approached, Pitcairn smiled sagely. "You have something urgent to discuss with me," he said. "I can see it in your eyes. Sit down."

"'I do," Finch said, lowering himself onto a stool. "I've received a dispatch from Colonel Prescott requesting that I march on Connecticut, to help him cut off a retreating Rebel army. Do you think you might lend me some men to deal with this threat?"

Pitcairn looked at Finch warily. "Prescott sent for you? I would think Governor Carleton would have ordered him to stay in Fort Ti after he liberated it from the Rebels. Sir Guy Carleton isn't one to order a pursuit lightly."

Finch cleared his throat. "I cannot pretend to know what Governor Carleton thinks. I simply have Colonel Prescott's request." He touched Pitcairn's arm. "Please, sir! Lend me a band of marines."

"Bah!" came a voice from a far table. "Don't lower yourself before them, Finch!"

Both Finch and Pitcairn turned. There, casually dining on sausage with his bare hands, his mouth half full, was Lord Dunmore.

Lord Dunmore placed what was left of the sausage on a plate, then made his way toward the two men. "My men are very much hoping to win some more glory, and they grow restless in this bitter cold. If you want a band of avengers who are out to win this war, you need look no further than my unpolished gems. A bit more training and we shall be able to join you in the march."

"The problem, sir," Finch said, "is that we have no time for further training. We need to march as quickly as possible. Tomorrow, if we can."

Dunmore nodded and licked his fingers. "Then we shall join you now. You have awakened in me a desire to lead these men to glory. I shall see to it that they make their mark in history."

Pitcairn stood up, shaking his head. "I am sorry, Giles, but I shall have none of this. It is all well to have a force of freed black men assisting our own as auxiliaries. But I do not condone them acting as free-roaming partisans with grounds for revenge."

"Nonetheless, Mister Pitcairn," Dunmore shot back, "the Ethiopian Regiment and Queen's Own Virginians are not your men to command. I shall leave the Queen's Own Virginians to you to do with as you see fit, but my friend Finch and I shall do some doodle hunting, shan't we Finch?" He clapped Finch on the shoulder.

"That we shall," Finch replied warily.

"This will be wonderful, don't you see, Finchy!" the governor crowed. "I know we have limited supplies of powder, but we can forage along the route for more. If Howe comes after us, what's the worst he can do? Send us home to our families? And if we succeed, we'll be heroes!"

"And what if the expedition fails?" Pitcairn said mildly, eyeing them both. "What if you are captured – or, worse, die?"

"Come now, Pitcairn!" Dunmore half-shouted. "No chance of that! You know as well as I that shooting an enemy officer is a hanging offense. As for our unlikely capture? As officers, the Crown shall be sure to ransom us from the hands of the Rebels."

Dunmore turned back to Finch. "Let me introduce you to Titus. He's not much to look at, but he's my ranking captain right now." Dunmore cupped his hands around his mouth and shouted across the room, "Hoy! Titus!"

The clicking of shoes sounded against the stone floor of the officers' mess. Finch and Pitcairn turned to see a young black man in his mid-twenties stand up from behind a table and make his way to the assembled group. Average in height, clad in a civilian hunting frock and a pair of roughly-fashioned trousers that were too big for him, Titus did not cut the most intimidating figure, but his gaze was steady and his jaw firmly set. *The question is*, the engineer thought, *will he and his men work alongside us and follow orders?*

Titus reached them and made a small, silent bow. "Colonel Finch," Dunmore announced, "this is Captain Titus, newly promoted from the rank of sergeant."

Titus inclined his head slightly but said nothing. Dunmore smiled. "I figured it might be fun to make some of the fusty old curmudgeons back at Horse Guards shudder, so I gave him a field commission."

Titus finally spoke. His expression was blank as he said in

a flat voice, "And how thoughtful of you for doing so, sir. You make me a charity case for your amusement."

Dunmore looked at him for a moment, then burst out laughing. "He's a wit, Finch! A wit!"

"That's entirely why you hired me, sir," Titus replied. He turned to Finch. "I escaped my New Jerseyan Quaker master's whip. Then I made my way to His Lordship's dominion in Virginia to fight on the Crown's behalf. I know I shall have my vengeance eventually, thanks to the governor here. He has offered me a convenient opportunity to advance my cause." He smiled, revealing gleaming white teeth.

"Your cause," Finch said. "Which is...?"

"Liberty for all slaves," Titus replied. "I'm not foolish enough to fight on either side for so trivial a reason as taxation." He pointed at Finch. "Colonel, your own King George abolished slavery in England not long ago. If Britain prevails, it will only be a matter of time before slavery is abolished here as well. I intend to speed up this time, whether by hook or by crook. That is my primary goal as a soldier. For now, however, my blade is yours."

Finch raised an eyebrow. Lord Dunmore laughed airily.

"Very well, Captain," Finch said. "You will be our third in command on this expedition. See to it that your men are disciplined. Take note of supplies and ammunition. Ensure that we have enough for our march."

Titus nodded. "Yes."

"Have your men seen combat outside of the assistance they rendered Major Pitcairn in Providence?"

Lord Dunmore wrapped his fingers around Finch's arm. "Of course, Colonel! By the time Admiral Howe relieved us, the Ethiopians and the Queen's Own Virginians had drilled under the marines of my personal vessel, the HMS *Fowey*, and—"

"From Captain Titus, please," Finch said stonily.

Titus cleared his throat. "With such training as skirmishers, we fought like the devil at Kemp's Landing. Launched a surprise attack from the trees. We captured many of our own masters and killed a number of other Rebels. We took on a job building a fort and breastworks on our side of Great Bridge. The Honorable Captain Charles Fordyce of His Majesty's Marines declared the works quite satisfactory." He grimaced. "Unfortunately, we were unable to use the defenses for their purposes, as we were called upon to launch an assault against what we thought was a lightly guarded fort on the Rebel side. Turned out to be more heavily guarded than we thought." He let out a harsh bark of a laugh. "We were then evacuated."

"Well, then," said Finch. "Let us join forces, that you may win more victories and avenge your defeat. Rally your men."

Forty minutes later, Finch stood before the Ethiopian Regiment and surveyed the nearly 300 men with a discerning eye. Most seemed in much better spirits and health than at the beginning of winter, and some seemed eager to partake in an adventure.

What intrigued Finch most was the intense look in many of the men's eyes. Finch could see that they were eager to go forth and fight – but whether it was for their rights and honor, for king and country, or for revenge, he could not tell.

Some of this eagerness melted away as Finch put them through a series of routine exercises.

"Prime and load!" Finch roared. He hoped to determine who would have difficulty following orders by having the regiment fire off a gun salute for Lord Dunmore.

Most of the men remained at attention, confused. Some, comprehending, took cartridges from their boxes and began biting them. Others, looking on, soon followed suit.

Finch shot a hard look at Dunmore, who stood beside him.

Lord Dunmore shrugged. "They were never trained to fire by command," he said. "Again, they were mostly used as skirmishers, firing at will."

"Ah," Finch replied. His attention returned to the men. Eventually, those who comprehended his orders managed to fire a salute – but Finch estimated that it took them almost a minute.

Finch shook his head. *Prescott had better be there to help these fellows when we arrive*, he thought. *Otherwise, this will be one brief expedition.*

Post Hill, New London, Connecticut

February 19, 1776, 8:04 AM

After several days' journey from Rhode Island, Finch stood at the foot of Post Hill, on a road at the edge of New London. "We shall rest at the hilltop," Finch roared to his soldiers. "Forward!"

"Sir?" came Titus' voice from behind Finch.

Finch turned. The captain was hurrying toward him, his brow furrowed in concern.

"Sir, our vanguard reports an approaching enemy militia force about a mile off. They comprise about 500 men. Your orders?"

A sizable regiment of trained militia. Damme. Finch pulled out his spyglass and scanned the horizon. He spotted the Rebels in the far distance, just to the west of the town. They looked menacing.

"To the trees!" Dunmore cried before Finch could stop him. "Let us not fight this day!"

Before Finch could issue an order of his own, the Ethiopians began scrambling for cover in the nearby woods. He opened his mouth to speak, but stopped when he felt a hand on his arm. He turned quickly.

Captain Titus stood beside him. "Sir, perhaps we should engage the enemy in combat. It would be one less unit to defeat when Washington comes along."

Finch smiled. "A fine point, Captain Titus!" he said. "We will be fighting the enemy regardless. It is best that we isolate them early. We must use the element of surprise." He pointed to a field just to the north of the woods. "Stand forth with four men in the open. Draw the enemy out. Keep the rest of the troops in the trees. On my order, fire as one."

Titus smiled and bowed. "Sir."

Post Hill, New London, Connecticut

February 19, 1776, 9:14 AM

From ten feet inside the woods, Finch watched as the militia captain gestured his company to a halt. Carefully, they surveyed Titus and his four handpicked men for a full two minutes, appraising their armaments. Then, alone, he urged his horse forward until he was directly in front of the four black men, who stood still and silent in the field.

The captain dismounted from his horse, then glared as he paced up and down the five exposed Ethiopians. "What's this? A band of armed Negroes wandering on their own? Can you explain yourselves, men?" The captain strode up to Captain Titus, then stopped directly in front of him and waited for a response.

Titus bowed his head. "Begging your pardon, sir. The master is travelling with us to New London, as he is hoping to establish a new farm there. We expect him to join us shortly.

We are to be his hands, bodyguards, and overseers. Can't be too careful in this time of civil war."

The Rebel officer placed his hands on his hips. "Overseers? What will you be planting?"

Titus smiled. "Well, sir, corn, pumpkins, beans—"

"Fire!" Finch shouted, then shot one of his pistols at the Rebel captain, narrowly missing him.

KRAKRAKRAKAKRAKRAK!

The Ethiopians positioned just inside the woods followed Finch's lead. Finch saw at least 15 militiamen fall in the first volley, screaming in shock and agony.

Seeing the Rebel minutemen beginning to form ranks into a battle line, Finch chopped his hand down. "Now, lads! Before they form up!"

Wailing and bellowing, the Ethiopians exploded from their positions in the woods. Finch smiled grimly as the minutemen gaped at them in surprise and terror. Some began to form ranks into a battle line; others stood motionless, too shocked to move.

As some of the Ethiopian soldiers continued firing, others drew knives and hatchets and charged the Rebel militia. The Rebels, caught entirely off guard, began to fall back.

Seconds later, the Ethiopians slammed into them, chopping and slicing into the Rebel flank.

Finch surveyed the battlefield with grim satisfaction as his men went about their gruesome business. Dunmore, safely perched atop a boulder, loudly cheered them on with great whoops of joy.

For a few minutes, the Rebel militia continued to fight as they withdrew. Five black Loyalists had fallen to the muskets of the minutemen and casualties continued to mount on both sides when the Ethiopians charged into the Rebels, cudgel meeting hatchet in a bloody melee. Then a musketball grazed the enemy officer's shoulder. Finch saw him grimace, then heard him grunt in pain. A moment later, he reined his horse around quickly and galloped off into the distance, leaving his men to die.

In time, the Rebel soldiers realized their commander had abandoned them. Hopelessness soon spread visibly through their ranks. Some fled; some continued to fight but were quickly overcome. Others fell to their knees, begging for mercy. Most were granted none, and blood flowed freely.

Lord Dunmore sidled up to Finch. "Did I not tell you that Titus was one hell of an officer, Mister Finch? Give us more officers like Titus, and we'll win the war tomorrow."

Finch silenced Dunmore with an upraised hand. "Yes, Governor, your captain did an excellent job. Now let us recall the men before we attract the attention of Washington and his column."

Still, Finch couldn't help but smile.

He hurried to where Titus was standing, surveying the final moments of battle. "Steady the men, captain, and recall them. We cannot have our men butchering those who have surrendered. Spare them, but encourage them to never again take arms against King George. We need to march to the top of Post Hill and wait for Prescott to arrive."

"Yes, sir," Titus responded grimly, still watching the battlefield.

"Well done, Captain."

Titus looked at him for a moment, sighed, and turned away once again.

Post Hill, New London, Connecticut

February 21, 1776, 2:17 AM

The winter hounded Finch's expedition, cold winds dogging their every step. Finch watched his men shiver, their bodies unused to these conditions. Although they were wrapped in blankets against the cold, they still struggled, many of them coughing and spitting.

In the days that followed their arrival at Post Hill, Finch and Lord Dunmore investigated the surrounding area, while Titus drilled the soldiers. There was not, as yet, any sign of a struggle, so it was very likely that Colonel Prescott's command had not yet encountered General Washington. In fact, the entire area seemed abandoned.

After two days of scouting the vicinity, Finch concluded that there was no trace of an army here. Concerned, he immediately ordered the packing of baggage. Something wasn't right.

Lord Dunmore airily brushed aside Finch's doubts. "Not to worry, Finch. Prescott's caravans must have been slowed. Or perhaps they came across some enemy skirmishers and gave chase. You have likely heard how Prescott can be quick on the pursuit. It is most unlikely that we have lost a whole column to the Rebellion."

Finch nodded. "Yes. It is also not likely that Prescott would call us here and then fail to show up. I'm beginning to suspect that the letter I received is not what it seemed."

"You have the letter, Finch, complete with the seal. It looked professional to me. Let us continue to wait. Our men are exhausted anyway and can use the rest."

And so they waited, resting the men a few more days. Finch spent much of the time worrying about the many possibilities that could have caused this unfortunate delay.

Meanwhile, Lord Dunmore, attempting to make himself useful, posted guards, inspected their poise, and tested the alarm.

On their fourth night at Post Hill, Titus and Finch sat before a fire, at times barely able to hear one another over the roaring wind.

"So, Captain Titus," Finch said, "should the Rebels find us before Prescott does, do we stand a chance?"

Titus sighed. "Even if we make our stand upon this hilltop, I would give us middling to poor odds, sir. Did you see how the locals looked at us as we passed? We are in Rebel country now. We don't know how much of Washington's wing will go after us, rather than Prescott, if it comes upon us." Titus took a long breath. "I understand the importance of this expedition, but I must say we executed it clumsily."

As sleet blew in his face, Finch could only nod grimly.

Post Hill, New London, Connecticut

February 25, 1776, 6:27 AM

Finch was abruptly roused from his slumber, and his dreams of home and family, by the raising of the general alarm. Fife and drum music brought him to his feet in a hurry. He pulled on his shoes and began reaching for his spyglass.

Then he heard it: the terrifying sounds of scattered musketry and steel on steel. The enemy was upon them.

Finch hurriedly clutched his spyglass, darted out the tent flap, and found the air choked with smoke. Stumbling over the newly dead and wounded, Finch scrambled to find Titus or Dunmore.

At length, he spotted Captain Titus about 50 feet away. In the midst of the smoke, Titus ordered his men to establish a line of battle around the hill's crest. There they crouched behind boulders and trees before letting loose with small crackles of musket fire. As they loaded, other soldiers behind them fired their muskets, allowing time for the front line to reload, while still pinning down the enemy.

Crouching low, Finch snuck up toward the front,

searching for the governor. Around him, many Rebel soldiers clad in blue, brown, and white uniforms, lay dead upon the ground. In front of him, others of their ilk turned tail and appeared to be retreating down the hill in a shaken order.

KRAK!

Another volley gusted into the Rebel unit's retreating backs, felling several more. A pang of guilt shot through Finch's belly. Normally, he did not condone firing on retreating men. But he was not about to raise the issue with Titus in the heat of battle.

Finch hurriedly surveyed the Crown soldiers through his spyglass. He could see that Titus was effectively orchestrating the maintenance of a strong, well-entrenched battle line. Finch knew enough to stand aside and let his captain lead his men.

Shots whizzed by overhead; one knocked Finch's hat off. Finch crouched instinctively, then shakily turned to get a better look at the enemy.

His heart sank. The Rebel soldiers numbered in the thousands, and were backed by at least a dozen cannon. They advanced on the Crown position with fife and drum, spoiling for a fight.

Washington's force. It was here.

Finch realized that the battle was already lost.

Dunmore, on the other hand, seemed ready to ride out the conflict to the end. "Steady, Ethiopians! Hold the line!" the governor cried, his face a bright red.

It was a pointless command. Cries of agony filled the air as the smoke on their far right flank cleared. Rebel regulars, having just volleyed, surged up that side of the hill, bayonets fixed and murder in their eyes.

Knowing they would be spared no quarter, the Loyalist blacks on the right broke ranks and fled.

"Every man for himself!" Lord Dunmore screeched, only now realizing his force's imminent doom. He pitched himself onto his mount and made an attempt to break through a thin, ever-closing ring of Rebel soldiers.

Finch stayed with his men as the Rebels rushed forward with a resounding cry of "Liberty!" He primed his two pistols and fired, but only managed to hit one fellow in the shoulder. The Rebel soldier dropped his weapon with a curse, but barely stopped to gather his courage before rushing forward once again.

"Break through the line, lads!" cried Finch. "It's our only chance!" He drew his saber and gestured wildly toward the Rebels, who were now pouring over the crest of the hill by the hundreds.

What was left of the Crown forces grasped their muskets with both hands far above their heads. Then they ran at the Rebels, hoping to shatter their discipline – and their skulls – with their weapons. The battle swiftly turned into hand-to-hand fighting.

Finch quickly surveyed the conflict once more. The Rebel lines were slowly moving to entrap the King's men. But after a few frenzied seconds of desperate searching, Finch found a hole in their formation.

"Hurry, lads! Now's our chance!" Finch shouted. "To the far left! Go!" He gestured his men forward.

As Finch led his soldiers toward escape, a young Rebel ensign suddenly blocked his path. He saluted Finch with his saber and held the Rebel battle standard in his other hand.

With a sigh, Finch drew his own saber and enacted a defensive guard, meeting the ensign's aggressive slashes with the forte of his blade.

The youthful ensign was strong, and he came closer to breaking Finch's parries with each successive blow. *Washington's Wing is closing in on us. I must end this quickly.*

Finch ducked a slash aimed at his head, then sidestepped the next thrust. He swiftly raked his blade across his antagonist's belly, spilling the entrails of the young man onto the battlefield.

Finch seized the battle standard as the Rebel soldier fell. He began running, attempting to bait the Rebels away from the Crown soldiers. "Got your flag, you scummy bastards!" Finch cried, cresting the hill and beginning to run down the other side.

Waiting for him was a brigade of Rebel soldiers.

Finch let his blade slip to the ground as the Continentals surged forth to disarm him. They grabbed and held his arms, confiscated his pistols, and snatched away the banner he had taken from the young ensign. Around him, Finch saw other Crown soldiers being seized and stripped of their weapons.

An imposing-looking Rebel militia officer strode forward. He stood close in front of Finch, his face only inches away. "I am Colonel William Burkett. You and your band of wayward Negroes have been placed in my care. You will all be treated fairly as prisoners of war. But cross me, and you shall be very sorry."

He turned to a corpulent man who was busily eating an apple while holding a spontoon. "Sergeant McFadden! Today, if you please!"

McFadden nodded and immediately stopped munching. He carefully impaled the apple on the blade of his polearm for safekeeping.

"Prisoner detail!" McFadden shouted. "You are now in the charge of the Northampton County Militia. We hereby consign you to confinement in Easton until parole or exchange. May God have mercy on your filthy souls."

chapter 7.
Imprisoned in Easton

April 25, 1776, 9:02 AM

Finch lay on the narrow bench in his cell, berating himself for the hundredth time for his foolishness, gullibility, and vanity. The expedition had been bound to fail from the beginning. Finch and Lord Dunmore had led their soldiers directly into a trap. The letter ostensibly from Prescott had obviously been a forgery – and the bait.

The war was over for Finch. He would spend the rest of it as a prisoner. And he might never see his family again.

True, the Crown had been known to exchange prisoners for some of their more promising officers – but "promising" hardly described Finch now. He would likely be left to rot.

Lord Dunmore had somehow escaped capture by Burkett and his soldiers. This was a mixed blessing. While it was good news that the Virginian governor would be able to continue to fight the war, he would not be happy to see his regiment dispersed – and General Howe would surely not be happy to learn that Dunmore had fled the field of battle and abandoned his own men.

Enough!

Finch opened his eyes and looked around his now-familiar cell.

It was small, solitary, and, to Finch's claustrophobic tendencies, panic inducing. Earlier in his internment he would have screamed for a guard, banging on the bars. By now, however, all the guards had grown tired of waiting upon their gentleman prisoner. For the past several days, they had ignored his noisy demands, leaving him to curl up in a ball and lose himself in his own thoughts.

Finch turned toward the wall and closed his eyes again.

Footsteps approached. Finch heard the distant sounds of a key in a lock and a clang as a prison door opened. By now, Finch knew that these sounds heralded the arrival of Sergeant McFadden as he sauntered menacingly through the cell block. Finch sighed and rolled over.

When McFadden appeared, he had a sickly and triumphant smile on his face.

"Alright, you! It's time to wake up. Come on, Colonel, sir!" McFadden shook the bars of Finch's cell from the outside.

"Ah, Sergeant," Finch said, sitting up. "What devious designs do you have for me today?"

"Interrogations," the sergeant replied with a smirk. "You don't think we'd offer you such excellent lodging in exchange for nothing, do you? Now, on your feet!"

McFadden led Finch to a small, cold, empty room in the basement of the prison. It was poorly lit by a pair of torches on either side of the door. In the dim light, Finch could make out a small wooden table with a chair on either side.

Wordlessly, McFadden pointed to one of the chairs.

As Finch made his way toward the table, he glimpsed the extensions of chains connected to manacles hanging from the wall. He sighed as he sat down. McFadden crossed the room and leaned against a wall. Together, they waited silently.

After a few minutes, there was a knock at the door. A voice on the other side said loudly, "Has the prisoner been brought in for questioning?"

"Aye, he has," McFadden shouted back.

The door opened, revealing Colonel Burkett, who appeared grim and determined. He looked Finch in the eye, doffed his tricorn hat, and stepped inside.

Burkett spoke softly. "Well, Colonel Finch, I hope you have found our hospitality pleasant. You will be staying with us some time longer. If you provide us with the right responses, we shall be sure to keep you very safe and happy here." He paused and placed his hat back on his head. "Without those responses, however, I'm afraid that your time with us will be decidedly less comfortable."

A sentry entered the room carrying a cloth bag. He handed it to McFadden, who drew out a cat-of-nine-tails. "Begging your pardon, Colonel," McFadden asked, "but what kind of answers do you seek?"

"Why, some simple verbal replies, nothing more," Burkett responded.

McFadden took the cat and brought it down on the table with a loud series of *thwaps*, each lash missing Finch by inches.

"Oh, stop that, McFadden. You shall not enact such measures toward our visitors. We should treat this gentleman with decency."

"Aye, sir," McFadden's replied. "I and Jezebel here will treat him with *much* decency. Feel free to go now, sir, if you wish. You have so many other matters to attend to. I have this one under control." He gestured toward the door.

The colonel seemed about to consent, but then shook his

head. "It is my duty to see this interrogation done properly. I shall ensure it is so. You may put the cat away."

McFadden's face fell. "So be it."

"Dismissed, Sergeant. Bring us some wine."

McFadden gave Finch a final sneer, then left the room.

Colonel Burkett smiled and began pacing around Finch, hands at his back. "Worry not, Finch, you are in good hands. We will not harm you so long as you tell the truth. It is a sin to bear false witness, after all." He paused, then leaned in close toward Finch's face. "In that vein, my gentle Colonel Finch, what brought you, at the head of a Negro expedition – and as an engineer, no less – to Post Hill and certain defeat?"

Finch took a slow, deep breath.

"Yes?" Burkett said. "Go on."

"In all honesty," Finch began, "I received a letter seemingly written by the hand of Richard Prescott, asking for military assistance. I decided to investigate the possibility of capturing your wing of men with the combined might of my forces and those of Colonel Prescott."

"Aha!" Burkett laughed. "Our ruse worked perfectly! I wonder if General Washington himself might promote me?"

Finch attempted to smile back. "It was a job well done."

"Glad you think so, Colonel. Tell me, is General Howe still leading you these days?"

"He certainly is," replied Finch. "Quite a gentleman – and very sympathetic to your cause, really. Though a consummate tactician, too."

"Well, it is a fine cause, in theory, after all," Burkett replied. "I can only hope that we shall truly achieve representation in parliament or a cessation of taxation. In truth, it seems that neither will be an easy fight."

"I agree," Finch replied. "And if by chance you do win this war, the Sons of Liberty had better make good on their promises of life, liberty, and property for all, lest I become very cross with them." He smiled tentatively.

Burkett snorted. "That will surely keep *me* up at night."

At length, a rather grumpy McFadden returned with a bottle of wine and two glasses. Burkett filled each glass half way and offered one to Finch. He took a sip. It wasn't bad.

"We do our best to treat our imprisoned officers well here," Burkett said. "Do tell me, the other white man you were with. Was that His Grace Lord Dunmore? His bonnet and kilt may have given him away."

"Aye," Finch replied, taking another drink of wine. "That was him alright."

"Ah, so those Negroes were his runaway slaves from Virginia?"

Damme.

Burkett glared at him stonily. "If we find out they are and that you did not admit them to be so, they will be much worse for wear than if you merely admitted as to their status."

Finch looked into the militia colonel's eyes. He saw much iron behind them. "Yes," Finch said sadly. "Lord Dunmore emancipated them through a proclamation not long ago."

Burkett considered the matter. "Every man has a right to life, liberty, and property. However, Father Nettles has often described the Negro as the tool of man, so who am I to disagree if he sees them as our belongings?" He held up his wine glass as if offering a toast. "Thank you, sir, for taking us one step closer to the return of stolen goods to their rightful owners."

Northampton County Prison, Easton, Pennsylvania

April 27, 1776, 6:07 AM

"Wake up, you! Wake up, you spineless compensator! I have good news for you."

Finch turned on his cold, hard bench and opened his eyes.

Before him, just inside his cell, stood Sergeant McFadden, his face twisted into a wicked grin. He took a dagger from his belt and twirled it smartly about his fingers. "Tell me, Colonel, is there something you'd like?"

"I'd like my men freed, Sergeant." Finch croaked, rubbing his eyes.

"Excellent to hear," McFadden remarked, then suddenly stabbed the dagger into the cell's small table. "Worry not, Finch. Your slave soldiers will not be imprisoned here forever. Our militia has recently closed a deal with the Virginians your Lord Dunmore stole from. The plantation owners they belonged to are on their way to take back the men, who will resume their duties for their masters." He grinned. "Isn't that lovely? We become rich, and your men go back to the plantations where they belong!"

Finch knew that, because he was an officer and a gentleman, the enemy was not permitted to touch a hair upon his head. Instead, McFadden took great delight in telling Finch things that the Rebels knew would infuriate him. Finch had no idea which of these things were actually true and which were as false as Prescott's letter. But he knew that all of the horrifying statements McFadden made were possible. The code of wartime conduct, which said that Finch could not be harmed, did not protect the many black soldiers Finch had commanded. According to reports from McFadden, Titus and his men had been brutalized, then locked away in cells without medical attention.

Damn these Rebel scum, Finch thought. *They call themselves freedom fighters? What about my men? Are they not the most oppressed of all?* Tears stung Finch's face as McFadden watched him with glee. *If I ever regain a field command, I will see to it that this prison is leveled.*

Northampton County Prison, Easton, Pennsylvania
April 28, 1776, 10:32 PM

Finch languished in his cell, pondering his ill fortune. He had tried in vain to devise any workable plan of escape. He eyed the bars wearily for the thousandth time, resigned to his routine of rest, food, and interrogation, knowing his men would soon be shipped home to bondage. The remorse weighed heavily on him.

Nothing had changed since yesterday. *Barred door with a little slot under which to slide a bowl of food? Check. Thick walls on all sides, excepting the blasted door? Indeed. Bowl of food with some bread, some stew, and a tankard of cider next to it? Still there. Latrine pail? Ugh, definitely still there. McFadden lounging in a chair in the guard's section of the cell block, slicing up an apple?* Finch listened, perked up, then sank down, disappointed. Yes. He could just barely hear the knife.

Finch lay back on his wooden bench, trying not to think of the family he had left behind, for fear of tears pouring down his cheeks.

As his gaze wandered over the bars to his cell, he paused at the last bar next to the keyhole. *Hang on a tick.* He rolled off his bench, crossed the cell, and examined the bars more closely. They were half-pin barrel hinges. Finch, ever the engineer, smiled as a plan began forming in his mind. *The proper application of strength at exactly the right angle just might enable him to lift the door free.*

Finch looked around wildly for an answer before his engineer's logic kicked in. *I'm going to need momentum, force, and just the right lever to pry that piece up.*

Suddenly, Finch's eyes went wide. He'd been sleeping on the answer all along. Finch's hands shook excitedly as he sprang toward the bench, grabbed it, and lifted it off the ground.

"What are you doing in there, Finch?" McFadden shouted.

Finch halted briefly. Catching his breath, he tilted the bench away from him and downward. Then he inserted one end of the bench under the bars, held it hard and fast in place, and very slowly, with much effort, pried the obstacles off the ground.

Success!

Finch grinned as he wrenched the bars open with a resounding squeal that echoed in the hall. He then hurried to put them back into place as he heard footsteps rapidly approaching.

McFadden suddenly appeared, scowling.

"What the blazes are you doing, Finch? If you aren't wailing like a banshee, you're trying to bring down the entire prison!" McFadden looked about the room suspiciously.

Finch smiled and lowered his head. "Just trying to keep myself entertained."

McFadden snorted. "By doing what?"

"Here," said Finch. "Let me show you." He pointed to the jail bars. "See there?" He strode over to them and touched them lightly. "Here's something interesting."

With a single, swift movement, Finch uprooted the loosened bars, then hurled himself out of the cell and charged the jailer.

Caught off guard, McFadden staggered backward a few steps, then clutched at Finch's shoulders. The two men fell loudly into the cell block hallway.

McFadden quickly recovered his composure and began throwing punches in Finch's direction. Finch desperately tried to block the cascade of strikes from McFadden's meaty fists, then suddenly dropped to the ground and rolled hard to one side.

Freed for a moment, Finch ran the ten feet to the guard's station, where a half-eaten bowl of stew sat on a small table. Finch grabbed the bowl and flung the hot contents at McFadden, who was hurrying toward him. As the jailer let out a shout, Finch smashed the clay bowl over the Rebel's head. McFadden groaned once, fell, and lay quiet.

Finch quickly dragged McFadden back into his cell. He stripped the man, exchanged clothes with him, and grabbed his keys. Finch then carefully replaced the cell bars and closed and locked the door. As he hurried down the hallway, he heard McFadden begin to stir.

Finch did his best to affect McFadden's confident swagger as he strode down the dark corridor, hoping to locate and perhaps free the Ethiopians. He passed one small, private cell after another and briefly gazed inside each one. All of the faces inside were white, and Finch did not recognize a single one. Occasionally Finch encountered another guard, but each simply waved or nodded at him half-heartedly, then went back to reading or whittling or staring out a window.

Then Finch looked out a window himself. The view revealed that he was on the second floor of a very long building, across a courtyard from another, similar structure. He continued walking.

After a few dozen more steps, he saw a narrow flight of stairs leading down. On impulse, he followed them down one flight, and then another.

At the bottom was another corridor that branched off in both directions. This hallway was dark and dank, and reeked of urine and sweat. Finch turned left and headed for what looked like a small pool of light, presumably shining in from an open window above.

Something moved in the darkness at the far end of the

hallway, beyond the puddle of light. Finch froze, then squinted, trying to make out a shape. Instinctively, he reached for his spyglass, then shook his head in self-disgust when his hand simply clutched at McFadden's rough militia uniform. Slowly, he continued down the fetid hallway.

Suddenly, the movement resolved into shapes that Finch recognized. Bodies. Dark bodies. Dozens of them, massed together behind thick bars in a single large room. Some of the bodies paced. Some shook. A few appeared to be praying.

Finch quickly looked around. He saw no one else.

"Captain Titus?" Finch hissed in as loud a voice as he dared.

No one heard him.

"Captain Titus?" Finch repeated louder, at a volume he immediately regretted.

A murmuring began from inside the cell, then turned into excited chatter—until a firm and familiar voice announced, "Silence!" After a pause, it said, a bit more softly, "Finch?"

It was the voice of Titus.

Then a different voice echoed down the corridor, from behind Finch. "I say, is that you, McFadden?"

Finch turned. About 20 feet behind him, mostly hidden in the shadows, stood a guard. Finch could not make out his face.

Unable to emulate McFadden's Scottish accent, Finch put on a Bostonian one. "Darwin, here," he replied. "I've been reassigned to help guard the Negroes. Congressman Patrick Henry of Virginia has demanded their return. We expect him to arrive at any moment."

"Very well," the guard shouted back. "I know that Colonel Burkett has a dispatch for the Congressman. I'll get it for you, and you can give it to him when he arrives."

"Yes, of course!" Finch said loudly.

The guard turned on his heel, walked off, and headed up the stairs.

For a few seconds, no one moved or spoke.

Suddenly, slow applause echoed in the distance, then began growing louder. Presently, four guards clambered down the stairs, clapping and nodding.

One of the guards made his way to Finch and stopped directly in front of him. "A valiant attempt, Colonel Finch," he said. "I especially enjoyed listening to your terrible effort at a Bostonian accent. But there has not been a Massachusetts regiment down here since the Seven Years War. Now, hand me the keys. I shall escort you back to your cell."

Finch turned and ran. He headed toward Titus and his soldiers, expecting to hear the roar of a musket and feel the sting of shot. Instead, he heard a voice say, "That's a colonel, you fool! Do you wish to be hung? We must chase him down!"

When he reached the pool of light, Finch saw that another corridor branched off to both the left and the right.

And on the right, a few feet from the corner, two Rebel guards leaned against the wall, their faces stretched into huge grins.

One of them stepped forward and quickly grabbed Finch by the throat.

"Colonel Finch," the guard said softly. "It appears that you have wandered off. Allow me to return you to your cell."

Governor Tryon's Mansion, New York City, New York
August 9, 1776, 2:58 PM

Squelch squelch.

It was a humiliating exchange. Finch and his Rebel counterpart walked the gauntlet of Monmouth County, New

Jersey. Soldiers on both sides stood at attention as the two men, blindfolded, were made to walk straight ahead toward their camps. Both factions stood ready to receive them under soggy flags of truce, with rain filling up their hats and sloshing over the sides.

Finch supposed he should have felt honored to be considered the equal of the famed partisan, John Stark. However, he also knew he should have never been captured in the first place, disgracing his nation and consigning Dunmore's Ethiopians to their fates.

"Halt!" a voice ordered.

Finch stopped walking and the blindfold was removed from his eyes. In front of him, a dozen Crown soldiers – all of them strangers – looked blankly at him.

An equally unknown captain appeared beside him. "This way, sir. Follow me." He led Finch for a few dozen steps toward a waiting carriage.

After riding for what seemed like hours, Finch was delivered to a dock on the Hudson River, where a flat-bottomed boat took him to New York City.

As he stepped out of the boat and began to walk the streets of Manhattan, Finch felt shaken, but otherwise at peace. When he passed the Queen's Head Tavern, he was hallooed and waved at by some of his fellow officers, who were lounging outside. Exhausted but happy to see them once more, Finch joined them.

"Welcome back, Finchy!" several officers cried. They clapped his shoulder, grasped his hand, sat him down, and ordered food and drink for him.

For the next hour, Finch did his best to answer their questions. "Did they treat you well?" "Are you glad to be back in action?" "Do you feel duly humbled, after ignoring orders?"

Eventually the questions became too much, and the

company became claustrophobic. Finch stood up and excused himself before his food arrived.

Finch walked on to the barracks. There, he dashed off a letter to Adelaide to inform her of his trials over the previous six months. Then, wanting to offer his respects and thanks to General Howe, Finch requested an audience with him, but he was coldly denied entry at the front gate.

"The general is otherwise occupied, Colonel Finch," the sentry replied smartly. "He will send for you when the time comes."

Despondent and lonely, Finch returned to the barracks. He spent the next day writing letters – first, another, longer note to Adelaide, expressing his love and longing for his family, then a letter to Pitcairn, apologizing for his misconduct in Rhode Island.

The next afternoon, while Finch was drinking tea, a messenger dressed in the uniform of the Thirty-Fifth Foot strode into the officers' mess and marched up to him. "Colonel Finch," he said sharply. "General Howe orders your immediate presence before him at his headquarters. Come with me, please, sir."

Finch nodded, put down his teacup, and rose. He followed the soldier out into the summer rain, where they sloshed to Howe's offices.

Once inside, he was regarded coldly by one of Howe's staffers. "The general has been expecting you, Colonel Finch," he remarked stiffly. "You're late."

"Apologies, Major. It was raining and—"

"Seat yourself. I will inform the General of your..." He sniffed his disgust at Finch's muddied uniform. "...presence in the building."

And so Finch waited, humming to himself in an attempt to keep up his spirits.

"Colonel Finch? You may come in now."

General Howe looked up from his writing as Finch walked slowly inside. The engineer doffed his hat and bowed, his shoulders slightly hunched.

"General Howe, sir, I humbly report for duty once more."

Howe glared at Finch, stonily looking down his spectacles.

"Finch. You've lost your touch. Taking on the role of a field commander. Allowing yourself to be tricked by obvious misinformation. Leading a full regiment to their death or capture. I even hear you attempted escape."

"Yes, sir. A few months ago."

The general sighed and removed his spectacles. "A most cowardly and dishonorable act. Britannia cares for her own, and you were taken fairly, through your own folly. The Rebels treated you well, I trust?"

Finch was stung by Howe's sharp words. "Yes, sir."

"Listen to me, Finch. We were to take the moral high ground. To barter with the Rebels. It is the only right and proper way to deal with such tragic occasions in war. In all honesty, I would rather have kept Colonel Stark prisoner, but Major Pitcairn and even General Clinton would not leave you to rot. You should thank them."

"Yes, sir. I will."

"I also received numerous dispatches from your wife pleading for your release. I must say, Colonel, she made a strong case for you. See to it that you do not lose her support."

"I shan't, sir."

Howe stood up. "Now, you had best make yourself useful, if you do not wish for me to call for your dismissal. There are depots that need building. Live up to your reputation as an engineer built by the words of your family and friends, and maybe I won't feel quite so foolish about releasing one of the Rebellion's most ruthless warriors in exchange for you."

Finch bit his lip. "Yes, sir."

"Dismissed, *Major*. And don't ever think about taking a field command again."

Finch flinched at his abrupt demotion, but if he showed a wounded expression, Howe did not acknowledge it.

A question then sprung to Finch's mind. "General Howe, sir. Many of my soldiers were taken captive after our skirmish with Washington's forces. Do we know what became of them?"

Howe waved his hand dismissively. "Returned to their homelands."

Finch's heart leapt. "To Africa?"

Howe looked at Finch with disbelief and disgust. "To their southern owners, Finch. Now, begone." He turned away.

Finch sighed. Of course. "They fought well on behalf of the Crown." Finch said. "They deserve to be honored, not imprisoned on plantations. The Rebels treated Dunmore's men like animals, sir. Surely they violated some code of conduct by mistreating our enlisted soldiers."

Howe shook his head without turning around. "Act like an animal, be treated like one. Your friends were in league with a villain who abused his power in the colonies. Lord Dunmore has been placed under house arrest for instigating their revolt. We shall win this war in a mannerly fashion. Be thankful you forced such good behavior from them when you commanded the men, Finch – else you, too, would have joined Governor Murray. Leave me."

Finch walked out of Howe's office into the thunderstorm outside. As rain poured over the tip of his hat, he sighed. *My family name has been disgraced, my command placed in bondage, and my King and country set back significantly.*

Finch reached for a pistol, only to remember that all his equipment had been confiscated by the Rebels. It was a further testament to his disgrace. *Then perhaps it is time for me to pay The Palisades a visit.*

Nodding grimly at the officers who greeted him as he passed, Finch walked the streets of New York, pondering his failures, until he came to the rushing river that flowed between Manhattan Island and New Jersey. He looked across the Hudson River at the fort atop New Jersey's towering cliffs, then at the river flowing swiftly below. His engineer's mind whirred with calculations.

That's a significant drop, Finch thought. *Simply striking the water from that height would easily kill me.*

A soft hand laid itself on Finch's shoulder. Then some blunt words were gently whispered into his ear. "Stand down, husband."

Finch jumped slightly and whirled about. Peals of laughter echoed around him.

There stood Adelaide in a simple but flattering blue dress. Standing beside her, grinning like a madman, was General Henry Clinton.

Clinton smiled and kissed Adelaide's hand. Finch looked on in amazement.

"Madam," General Clinton said, "allow me to present your husband, Major Giles Finch. We'll make a colonel of him again soon enough, I should think!"

"A-Adelaide?" Finch stammered, simultaneously stunned and overjoyed.

A moment later, their children poked their heads out from behind Adelaide. Caroline ran to her father and hugged him.

Adelaide smiled warmly as she cupped Finch's cheek. "It is good to see you up and about once more, husband. We heard from Pitcairn about your heroic, if foolish, stand and imprisonment, so we decided to return to the colonies, work toward your release, and offer you our support and love, at a time when the Crown would lend you little." She laughed and took Finch's hand. "I am still surprised that General Howe listened to my pleas and those of General Clinton and Major Pitcairn. His letters sounded angry enough to kill when I first approached him. You really oughtn't to have gone on that sortie. It was an obvious trap."

Before he could respond, Constance also ran to Finch and hugged him. "I'm just glad you're home, father."

Caroline declared, "I hear the Rebels eat their captives. Papa, I am ever so glad you're safe!"

Archibald, shy as ever, peeked out from behind his mother's skirts and waved.

Clinton laughed and patted his belly. "Well, isn't this a sight! What a fine family reunion! I take it you and your children will be staying in the colonies sometime longer, then, Missus Finch?"

"W-well, I do not know—" Giles began uneasily.

Adelaide interrupted him. "Of course!" she said brightly. "We are here to support my husband and attend to his camp until the war's end. Worry not, dear, Gus is fine. We left him in the capable care of your brother after he proved somewhat restless on the voyage to England, and—"

Finch found his voice at last. "Now, Adelaide—"

"Come now, Finch!" Clinton said, grinning. "Your woman has come all this way, and you're going to spurn her company? You must be colder than I thought!"

Finch blushed madly. Adelaide took his hand. "Come Giles, let us showcase to the world our love for one another. We are family; we must stand together through all the difficulties and delights life will hurl at us."

Finch pondered the offer. Howe was offering him a chance to do what he truly loved – benefit the colonies by building, rather than destroying. What's more, he was again with his family, who stood loyally by his side.

Things were not so terrible after all.

And, perhaps, he might one day redeem himself and avenge the defeated Ethiopian Regiment.

Finch took Adelaide's hand. Suddenly, a memory of music filled his ears. "Dance with me?"

Adelaide curtseyed gracefully. "Of course, Giles."

Finch pulled her close.

They moved in tandem, his arm on her back, their feet gliding over the cobblestones, as Adelaide hummed a melody. Suddenly, Finch was transported back to Germany and the court of Frederick the Great, where he and Adelaide had first met. Now the name came to him without effort.

"Suite Number 2," he whispered into Adelaide's ear. "The minuet movement in B-Minor. Bach."

"Exactly, my beloved," she whispered back.

Giles Finch will return!

Parting Shots

And so, my dear readers, the first book in this collection that is The Finch Folio concludes at last.

Finch has been returned to his family, able to once more serve his king and country. And though his status is somewhat reduced, some satisfaction yet abides.

Will Finch regain his Colonelcy? Perhaps he shall surge beyond it? This would be all very well, but what of the Ethiopians? Of the Southern Front? Of the very wellbeing of the colonies at large?

To those patient enough and content to wait, to those imaginative enough to keep an open mind as I weave my tale, some of this may yet be revealed in the next volume of this – The Finch Folio.

With warm regards, I thank you most sincerely for partaking in my book, and remain, humbly your servant,

—Daniel H Lessin

About the Author

A native of New Jersey and resident of Minnesota, Daniel H Lessin has a History degree from Carleton College and is a seasoned Revolutionary War re-enactor. Besides writing books, Daniel enjoys the company of animals (especially dogs), board game design and figurine wargaming, computer gaming, and partaking in rituals with his Reformed Druids of North America grove.

Acknowledgments

With special thanks to:

Madhav Ajjampur

Gilah Benson-Tilsen

Sanda Cohen

Christopher Culler

Carl Duff

Scott Edelstein

Alexander Farrell

Patti Frazee

Ralph Fuhrmann

Jason Grossman

Carrie Harshbarger

Veronica Hatala

George Hill

Amber Johnson

Deb Johnson

Elizabeth Motich Gross

Jennifer Munnings

William North

David Oppegaard

Anne Osberg

Sarah Ravely

Jacob Waldman

Antoine Watts

Naida Wharton

Ralph Wharton

Serena Zabin

The Royal Provincial 4th Battalion, New Jersey Volunteers Reenacting Group

And many thanks to countless others for their contributions to the Finchverse.

CPSIA information can be obtained
at www.ICGtesting.com
Printed in the USA
LVHW051227141020
668673LV00006B/530

9 781734 797602